COVEN LEADER

Book Nineteen of the Hayle Coven Novels

PATTI LARSEN

Find out more about Patti Larsen at **pattilarsen.com**

chapter one

So weird, this image of me reflected back from the mirror. I'd wanted cream or even a color, but Mom and Shenka—and all the other women in my life who thought they had a say—insisted on white.

I wasn't an angel. But as I stood there, looking at myself in my wedding dress, I smiled.

And felt like one.

Slow breathing did wonders for the wild pounding of my heart as Mom lifted the lace veil and pinned it to the back of my piled curls. Tears glistened in her eyes as, with trembling hands, she released the fall of soft fabric , the sigh of it behind me like the exhale of all the sadness I'd ever felt. Gone with the excitement of what I was about to do.

I fidgeted a little with the skirt of my gown, loving the halter style, the way the dress clung to me in shining folds of satin. While I knew Mom would have preferred to dress me in a princess concoction of froth and poof, I'd won this argument.

Mostly because I didn't give her a choice and just went to the local bridal boutique and bought it without telling a soul.

"Perfect choice," Mom said with a sweet smile as she smoothed a dangling curl back from my bare shoulder. "You are so beautiful."

I turned in a rush and hugged her, not caring if my dress crumpled, if my hair and veil suffered. "Mom," I whispered, doing my very best not to cry. "Thank you."

She waved one hand in front of her face when she let me go, cheeks pink, laughing through sparkling tears.

"Don't you dare," she said. "You'll ruin your makeup."

Tastefully applied, thanks to Shenka, who stood back with a beaming smile, her knee-length dress the perfect shade of family magic blue.

"Miriam's right," my second said with a hitch in her voice. "You're gorgeous, Syd."

I felt gorgeous. Turned to look at myself again, catching the glitter of my engagement ring in my reflection. Liam presented me with the large diamond the very night I proposed, a ring, it turned out, he had in his possession for almost a year.

Imagine that.

I smiled, focusing on right now. Refusing to allow the craziness of my life to intrude for this one lovely, perfect evening. The sun had already set and I knew the rest of the wedding guests and party would be arriving any minute now the vampires were able to join us.

Shenka touched up Mom's eyes as I sat on the edge of the bed and watched, smiling as they spoke in low, soft voices, giggling together over something I missed. Because my mind, traitor that it was, had already drifted elsewhere.

I still found it hard to believe it had only been two weeks since conclave. Even more difficult to believe Mom allowed thirteen days to go by before she married me off. I was sure, that first morning Liam and I made our announcement, she'd have us out in the back yard, calling for an officiator the second she saw the sparkly on my finger.

But she showed amazing restraint and, considering the Council was now happy I was getting married, it might have been the fact the pressure was off her shoulders granting me even a short bit of breathing room.

I shouldn't have been surprised the wedding came together so quickly. Shenka being the mistress of organized, after all, must have had a plan already in place, mobilizing the coven into immediate action. And because our family had such diverse interests—from photographers to bakers to florists and part-time musicians—the entire process was covered and arranged before I could say otherwise.

Just as well, considering how bad I was at keeping track of details. Or running my own life, let alone a wedding. I'd been part of Sunny and Uncle Frank's, but my involvement stopped at trying on dresses and shoes and arranging Sunny's bachelorette party. Which I'd forgotten all about. Leaving it to Mom and her old second, now my rep on the Council, Erica Plower to save my forgetful butt.

At least nothing blew up in the past two weeks, alliances formed during conclave still holding together. The new European Council Leader, Femke Svensson, suggested Steam Union members be assigned to the various Councils and, in doing so, ensured the safety of most sorcerers as well as serving as protection against the Brotherhood.

I still waited on word from her about my vampire friend, Sebastian DeWinter. She promised to look into the Pannera Sthol issue, now aware the undead queen was under the thrall of the taint introduced by the dark sorcerers. She was also informed Sebastian, the legitimate blood clan leader, was trapped and most likely being tortured by my former Hayle coven member turned undead spy for the Brotherhood, Celeste Oberman.

What I wouldn't do to get my hands around her neck and squeeze. She'd been a thorn in my side for years now and yet always remained outside my grip. But I had a feeling, once Femke gave me permission to act, Celeste's days of irking me would end in a short walk to a tall stake and a very, very hot fire.

Couldn't wait. I'd bring marshmallows.

The fact the Brotherhood went to ground did nothing to make me feel better. Even though my friends and allies were making the sorcerer's lives here on this plane almost impossible—instant death, if caught, could be an excellent deterrent to making their presence known—I knew the threat Liander Belaisle and his sect presented was far from over.

With his possession of the stronghold and the empty plane Mom's Enforcers once called home, Belaisle was in full control of the site where our last battle was meant to be fought. Ameline Benoit, my nemesis, had been right when she said it didn't matter who held possession. And the whole power source issue. According to Eva Southway and the other Steam Union members, the stronghold could offer Belaisle some serious backup in a fight.

Still, when the day came, we'd be there to meet Belaisle no matter what. But it bugged me knowing I'd be walking into a situation he controlled rather than the other way around.

Sigh. I had to force my hands into stillness, the constant twisting of my new ring a habit I'd picked up to add to the others I fell into when my churning mind took over. At this rate, I'd either rub my finger raw or thin the platinum band to nothing before I even made it down the aisle.

Couldn't help it. Thinking about the last battle made me worry over Ameline and her power shortfall. Which pushed my mind toward my sister. Ameline already demanded I turn over Meira's demon magic to her so she could complete her journey to maji. The resounding "NO" I'd delivered didn't seem to have fazed Ameline's plans. Which meant my almost constant worry about Meira surfaced about as often as any of my other nibbling anxieties.

A lot, in other words.

Meems insisted she was fine, that all was well. Our daily talks reassured me this was true. And knowing my demon grandmother, former Ruler Ahbi Sanghamitra was embedded in the Node power source keeping Demonicon stable made me feel a little better. Her spirit was part of the veil Ameline would be forced to cross if she wanted to go after Meira.

But Ahbi wouldn't be much help if Ameline went after my sister while she was here on my plane.

I must have been frowning, because the giggling pair went silent. The sudden quiet snapped me out of my thoughts, raised my eyes to see them watching me with irritation.

"You," Shenka shook an eyebrow pencil at me, "are going to be happy tonight or I'm going to kick your butt."

Mom nodded once, definitive. "Me first," she said.

I swept away my thoughts with a mental sweep of a broom and smiled at both of them. "Sorry," I said. "Just keep me distracted and I'll be fine."

Mom rose and came to me, taking my hands, pulling me to my feet just demon power surged downstairs.

"That would be your sister," Mom said. "And your father." Her voice wavered just a little, her smile a bit too bright. "Are you ready?"

A flutter of butterflies woke in my stomach, rising to beat themselves against my ribcage in response.

Was I?

Mom turned before I could answer, fished a bottle of perfume from the back of my drawer. I laughed, remembering she'd left it for me. Lilac, her signature. I shook my head when she offered it up.

"I think I need to find my own," I said. "He'll just have to smell me as I am for now."

Shenka hugged me, pressing her cheek to mine. "Liam will be in such a daze when he sees you, his brain won't be functioning anyway."

I laughed nervously, dancing insects increasing their pace. "I'm going to throw up."

Shenka pulled back and grinned. "This from a woman who has faced death, destruction, mayhem and almost certain collapse of a plane or two."

That was different. In fact, I'd rather face a horde of Brotherhood than the aisle waiting for me in the back yard.

Running sounded good about now. Gulp.

Shenka winked. "I have a bucket out there," she said with glee. "Just in case."

Oh. My. Swearword.

Another rush of power broke through the family wards, spirit magic tied to the undead. I turned to the door as it creaked open after a quick knock, and opened my arms to my sister as Meira and Sunny entered. She wore her human persona tonight, my height, no giant platform boots in sight, her strapless dress a match for Shenka's, only hers in the deepest amber.

"Gorgeous," she said. "Liam's going to drop."

Another nervous giggle escaped me, paired with the sudden need to sprint through the door as Charlotte entered, her wolf spirit in her eyes. I squeezed her, too, feeling certain I'd be all hugged out by the time tonight was over.

Charlotte wore an iridescent fabric, shimmering with a soft gold sheath of gauze over top. Mom's brilliant idea made me smile as she dressed each of my bridesmaids in their magic colors. Sunny's stunning face shone with joy as she squeezed me, silver gown tightly fitted to her perfect body.

Finally, Trill entered, shy and, from the way she walked in her heels, more than a little uncomfortable. But her deep crimson dress was the perfect color for her.

The girls all gathered to admire each other's outfits, the first time they'd all been together since Shenka started putting this dog and Persian show together. I stepped aside, let them ooh and ahh over each other as the door creaked one last time and Dad poked in his head, blue eyes and tanned skin of his human persona firmly in place.

"It's almost time," he said, deep voice rumbling in the sudden silence. "But I'd like a moment alone with the bride, first, please."

My bridesmaids and maid of honor—Meira, naturally—all left in a flutter of brilliant dresses and laughter. Mom was last to go, pausing beside Dad, one hand reaching out. But, just before she could touch him, she let her hand fall as she ducked her head and disappeared out into the hall.

I couldn't help the soft sigh of sadness escaping me. Dad sighed, too, broad shoulders sagging in his black tux. "I'm sorry, cupcake," he said. "I didn't want to ruin your night."

I went to him, hugged him, felt the warmth and strength I remembered from my childhood, laughed at the nickname I used to hate and now adored.

"Dad," I said, "I'm so glad you're here."

He leaned back after a moment, his eyes damp, handsome face smiling as a flicker of amber danced through his gaze. "All your mother and I ever wanted was for you to be happy," he said. "Are you, Syd?"

I stopped, drew a breath. Thought about running one last time.

Asked my heart.

Already knew the answer as my itchy feet calmed, my pounding heart falling into a softer rhythm.

"Yes, Dad," I said, amazed to believe it. "I am. As happy as I think I'll ever be."

He bent and kissed my forehead. "Then I'm happy for you," he said. "Are you ready?"

Mom's question again.

I nodded, paused. "I just need a second."

Dad left me with a soft squeeze of my hand. "I'll be right downstairs," he said.

Left me alone.

I turned one last time to look in the mirror, at the woman I'd become, the bride I was. Hugged myself as the diamond ring flashed and a trail of tears escaped to track down my right cheek.

We love you, my vampire sent, her magic flowing around me.

We will always be here for you, my demon's graveled growl went on as amber fire lit my insides.

No matter where life takes you, Shaylee sent, Sidhe green

flaring within, *we are one, forever.*

The family magic swirled in joy while my maji power stirred. Even the black flower of my sorcery answered, blossoming a moment before falling still.

Thank you, I sent to all of them, pulling myself together. *I love you, too. And would be nothing without you.*

But it wasn't their love I longed for, wept for. My hand trembled as I lifted it to look at the diamond on my finger, fighting the face trying to rise in my mind. The feel of magic I'd loved and lost. The taste of chocolate and the heat of power.

I loved Liam. We would be happy together as long as he lived.

And I refused to think of anyone else.

A tissue cleared up the moisture, a soft dab with a cotton stick erasing the moment of weakness.

All right, Sydlynn Thaddea Hayle.

Time to get married.

I left my reflection behind with my longing and sadness and closed the door firmly behind me.

chapter two

I paused at the top of the stairs, listening to the laughter and chatter going on below. The warm evening enveloped me as I stood there in the dark of the landing and absorbed the happiness of my family and friends.

Okay then. Show, road, hit it.

I drifted downstairs, grateful for the low-heeled shoes Shenka sighed over but finally agreed to let me wear. Heels would have killed me, the condition I was in, as the butterfly hop was in full swing all over my insides again with no hint their little party planned to wrap up anytime soon.

I was ready. But that didn't mean I was allowed to be all calm and dignified about it.

Someone had turned out the hall light, probably to hide the wedding party from the gathered guests milling about in the back yard. It was decorated much as it had been for Sunny and my Uncle Frank's wedding, soft lights and floating panels of gauze. But a heavy blue carpet replaced the red one the undead couple used, and the points of decoration were in all colors of magic.

Nice touch.

I hesitated at on the bottom step, turning from the talking group in the living room to the hall beside me. The closed door by the staircase. I tried talking to Gram earlier this morning, but she refused to say a word to me. Hadn't spoken to me since I announced my engagement to Liam.

I knew why. Gram didn't think he was the right one for me. And yet, it wasn't just my sweet Gatekeeper she held against me. Her bitterness over her own failed love and the loss of her magic after fighting so hard, giving up so much, layered on top of her disappointment in my choice.

Gram had been my anchor, her power and mine intertwined for so long not having that connection anymore was one of the hardest things I'd ever had to deal with. Worse was feeling Gram's power inside the one person I hated the most and I swore to myself, the moment this thing with the Brotherhood was over, I was killing Ameline personally before returning Gram's magic to her.

I wanted my grandmother back.

That's why it hurt me so much she refused to talk to

me. To interact at all.

To come to the wedding.

I had to try one last time. Maybe seeing me dressed like this, in my white dress, if I appealed to her heart, she'd cave. Because I really wanted her with me.

Selfish? Yeah. Guilty.

I eased Gram's door open, slipping inside, a little surprised to find it unlocked. A momentary hope rose. Maybe she'd changed her mind, was already out there, with the others. Waiting for me to appear.

But no. I spotted her almost immediately, sitting on the floor on the other side of her bed, only the wispy bits of her hair floating over the edge of the quilt letting me know she was there.

Hunched, hugging her knees as usual, staring out the window with her faded blue eyes.

I usually sat next to her when I tried to talk to her, but the dress made it impossible, not to mention the floor-length lace veil. Instead, I took a seat on the small chair next to her dressing table and folded my hands in my lap.

Stared at her for a while.

Touched her with my magic.

She flinched away, turning her head, her back, spinning sideways so only her hunched shoulders under her thin sweater were visible.

"Gram," I whispered, more tears rising, these choking

me. Leading to an ugly cry. Shenka would kill me for messing my makeup. "Please."

She refused to answer, what little magic she had left closed off and dark.

I couldn't make her attend. Would never do that to her, anyway.

"I love you," I said. Rose and went to her, bending to kiss the top of her head. "No matter what. Soul sister."

She grunted, shrugged me away.

And I left. But not before I caught the faint sound of her weeping.

Damn it.

I didn't know he was there until Sassafras's body brushed against my legs on the way out.

"Just give her time," he said, looking up at me from where he sat on the hem of my dress, fur blending into the fabric. "She's struggling still."

I bent and lifted him into my arms, cuddling him close as he purred against me.

"Thank you for taking care of her," I said, throat still tight. Sighed deeply. "I can't cry."

He head-butted my chin. "Then don't, silly," he said. "It's your wedding night."

I set him down, watched him sashay his silver butt into the living room. Heard Dad laugh, Sunny's tinkling mirth joining his.

Knew I just couldn't join them yet.

I needed a minute. Maybe an hour? How about a few years?

I rushed down the hall and into the kitchen to catch my breath and slow the wild beating of my heart. I thought I was over this?

Since when did I ever make anything easy for myself?

My hands white-knuckled over the back of the chair I grasped for support as I forced air in and out of my lungs. It was all coming together so fast, like a freight train bearing down on me. The butterflies now had giant wings, so crowded in there I was certain, at any second, I would puke all over my pretty white dress.

Yup yup.

My egos embraced me with power, soothed me, pulled me back from the brink of crash and burn. Enough so when I felt Enforcer magic cross the wards and come to the kitchen door, I didn't freak out.

But breathing became very hard all over again.

Quaid let himself in. Seemed surprised to find me standing there alone, staring at him. He froze, one hand on the doorknob, one foot over the threshold, his chocolate eyes locked on me.

If it wasn't for the fact my hitchhikers were already alert and on duty, I'm sure I would have lost it. Fallen to my knees and cried like a baby, run to him, something.

Probably something stupid I'd regret the rest of my very, very long life.

Instead, I stood there, held in place by their supporting power, even my demon's normal need for him dampened by her determination to keep me upright and functioning.

Quaid's face flashed through shock to hurt to bitterness as he closed the door behind him. Took a step toward me. Stopped.

"I can't believe you're marrying him," he said.

Had he said anything else like, "Hi, Syd, nice night, right?" Or, "Wow, you look amazing." Or even, "I'm starving, want to grab a burger?" Anything else. I know I would have been in his arms and gone.

Long gone.

But his anger lit mine like a wild fire out of nowhere.

You know I have a temper, right?

My demon snarled, her power snapping against him as Shaylee shook the house. Just a little. My vampire's power sizzled over his shielding in tiny lighting bolts of fury while the family magic, twice rejected by him, hummed its unhappiness.

My sorcery blossomed, begging to be fed.

My luck, he'd probably give us heartburn.

"How dare you," I snarled, straightening as my fury jammed an iron rod down my spine. "You have the nerve to come here after lying to me over and over again. After lying to *her*." How many times had he told me there was nothing between him and Payten, his little Enforcer

17

friend? How many times? And yet, here I found out, from her no less, she worried he was cheating on her. His girlfriend.

With me.

And he had been, the unfaithful bastard.

Quaid's face tightened with fury. "I have no idea where your fixation with Payten comes from," he said. "But for the last time, Syd, she and I were never together."

"Go tell her that," I snapped. "She was pretty convinced otherwise." Was that confusion on his face? Didn't matter. "You've made your choice," I said. "You joined the Enforcers." I still ached inside from the recoil of family magic when he'd chosen the order over me. "I'm tired of your endless revolving love. I need someone who is here for me, no matter what. Someone I can be there for, too. And that someone has never been you, Quaid." I turned my head as hurt flashed over his face. "Time to move the hell on. Like I have."

Now who was the liar?

Quaid didn't get a chance to say anything, though I could feel him swaying toward me, saw him lift his hand to me out of the corner of my eye.

Because the moment he did, Dad strode into the room, his power pulsing with anger.

"Quaid," he said, demon power a thundering undercurrent, "it's time for you to leave."

I felt his hesitation, turned back to watch as Quaid dropped his head, shoulders sagging, and spun toward the door. Almost called out to him, had to bite my lower lip to stop myself as he firmly closed the door behind him.

Dad's hands guided me around, his arms embracing me as I trembled against him, my heart numb.

"Are you all right, cupcake?" Dad leaned back, anger still snapping in his eyes. "That boy has about all the sense of the Demoniconian ruling family."

Which wasn't much. Made me giggle, nerves and anger and sadness all conspiring against me.

"Dad," I whispered. "What am I going to do?"

He shook me, just a little. "Do you love Liam?"

I nodded. Was all I could manage.

"Do you want to marry him tonight?"

Eep. "I have a choice?"

Dad sighed. "You always have a choice," he said. "No matter what anyone tells you. What did I say upstairs?"

"You want me to be happy." I felt so little standing there with my father, like a girl who lost her way.

"Exactly." Dad let me go. "Now, you tell me. What do you want to do?"

I thought of the family, waiting. Of the girls in their dresses. The Council and my responsibilities. Of Mom and Gram. Quaid and love lost. And, finally, of Liam.

My oak tree. Strength unseen, roots running deep beneath him. Courage and kindness and a heart so open it was no wonder I loved him. Really.

"I want to get married," I said.

Dad's smile softened the last of his anger. "Your wish is my command," he said. "Which means, to answer your question, you're going to take my arm," he offered it to me, "and we're going to go out there," he turned me toward the hall and began to walk me out, "and you're going to say I do to a young man who loves you."

As if in response to Dad's words, the soft sound of music floated past the living room from the hall to the back door. Calling me onward.

Right then. No more interruptions.

To hell with Quaid. I was going to be happy with Liam if it killed us, damn it.

chapter three

I stood at the back of the giggling line, forcing myself to smile as the girls turned and waved at me. Trill went first, flowers clutched in her hands like a lifeline. I grinned, a real one, at the sound of hooting from who had to be Apollo, her inappropriate brother, and thanked him silently for breaking my funk.

Sunny went next, Charlotte behind her. Mom waited with Meira as Shenka strode out with her shoulders back, confident in her high heels.

Meira saluted me with her bouquet before heading off after the others. Weird, it felt surreal, almost like it was just Uncle Frank and Sunny getting married again. Except, this time, I was the one in the white dress.

Mom took my free arm, not looking at Dad. I looked back and forth between them, heart sad, asking myself for the millionth time if this was worth it.

My Steam Union friend, Piers Southway, didn't seem to think love was a good reason to get married. And considering the fact the man I loved the most just walked out without trying to fight for me... not fair, I guess, since Quaid made his decision a long time ago.

Still, what was I doing? Setting myself up for heartbreak?

But as my brain burned over those thoughts, I felt myself shake them off. No. There was nothing saying Liam and I would end in disaster. That we wouldn't have a good life together, no matter he would die long before me, thanks to my immortality. I would love him and enjoy him for as long as I had.

And I would be happy to be his wife.

Mom kissed my cheek softly before smiling, lower lip trembling.

"Are you ready?"

"Let's do it," I said.

And walked out into the back yard with a confidence I didn't feel and a new selection of butterflies making merry just at the base of my throat.

As my foot crossed the threshold, Sassafras's silver body streaked past us. The moment his paws touched the blue carpet, though, he slowed to a dignified waddle, nodding to the gathered guests as he made his way to the front of the aisle created in the yard.

I kept my eyes fixed on him, happy for a little

distraction, as he leaped up onto the special platform created just for him and turned, fluffy tail wrapped around his paws, amber fire in his eyes. Mom, Dad and I proceeded down the carpet to the strains of wedding music.

With every step, my panic increased until I knew, if I opened my mouth, a flock of very colorful insects would fly out just before I upchucked every single thing I'd ever eaten. I barely saw any of the faces turned toward me, my head echoing with the sound of the song marching me to my doom.

My eyes flickered around in anxious need, awkward smile plastered to my face as my desperate need to escape returned in a wash of Oh. My. Swearword.

My vampire's soft laughter and the touch of her power helped calm me, enough I started looking around for somewhere to run. My demon grumbled, her magic burning through the fear clutching my throat. Shaylee's soft singing eased me further, the family magic buzzing softly, shimmering inside me in tune to my maji power.

I could just turn around and go back inside. What could they say? Nothing. I'd lock my door and tear open the veil. Or I could do that right here. Ahbi would welcome me to Demonicon, wouldn't she? Of course she would. Perfect. Time to get the hell out of—

Hazel eyes sparked with green, wide and wet with tears. The moment I met Liam's gaze, all my fear dissolved, my anxiety dying away. The expression on his face, the way his body leaned toward me as I approached, filled me with a rush of love so powerful I almost sobbed.

Instead, I felt my cheeks relax, my lips curve into a heartfelt smile, my body unwind from my tense need to flee. Anywhere, that was, but into his arms.

I hardly noticed Varity Rhodes standing beside him, the old Enforcer Leader and dear friend of Gram's here to officiate the ceremony. Not when Liam reached for me as Dad let me go, his big hand taking mine while Varity said something about magic and releasing me.

Mom's power touched me, Dad's at the same moment.

"I free my daughter to wed," Mom said.

"I free my daughter to wed," Dad repeated.

And then it was just Liam and me. And the words we had to say, the magic we had to share.

I could have made other choices, could have wed for politics or not at all and, instead, give up leadership of the coven, if that was what I really wanted.

But standing there, holding Liam's hand, feeling his love like an endless river, his strength the power of an ancient oak tree eager to give me shelter, support and all the goodness of his kind heart, I knew I couldn't have made a better choice.

chapter four

I leaned to the side as Varity began, bent and kissed the top of Galleytrot's head. The giant black hound sighed, red fire in his eyes dying as he sank to his haunches, tongue lolling out in a happy doggy smile.

Happy wedding day, he sent.

Thank you, I answered, calm at last, stomach settling into quiet. *I worried you didn't want us to go through with it.*

I just wanted to be sure you wouldn't hurt him, the big hound's mind rumbled like a thunderstorm in the distance, the scent of spring rain reaching me. *That you wouldn't change your mind at the last minute.*

My eyes returned to Liam. *Not a chance*, I sent.

Not now. Not ever.

Varity was mercifully swift, the ceremony rather painless, though I remembered little of it afterward. The vows done, a pair of rings firmly on our fingers, I took Liam's hands in mine and opened up the family magic to him.

"Welcome, Liam O'Dane," I said, the coven's power linking to him, making him a part of our union of souls, adding the richness of his Sidhe energy to the family magic. I felt his power embrace me, the joining of our magicks tingling at the edges a moment before he came through, loud and clear, in the flow of the family power. "To the Hayle coven."

He bowed his head. "I'm honored to be a member of such a powerful family," he said, "and will take my duties both as your husband and as a member of this coven seriously and treat it and you with the utmost respect."

Nice little speech, I sent. *Practice it much?*

His mind laughed in mine, our connection all the more powerful now he had family power to back him up.

Naw, he sent with a casual air. *Something I tossed off just now. So kind of you to approve, Coven Leader.*

Smartass husband, I sent. *Watch it.*

"Are you going to kiss him?" Varity's evil grin made me blush. "We're waiting."

Groan.

Liam didn't hesitate, hands sliding over my face, the coolness of his gold wedding band leaving a trace of sensation across my skin as he bent and pressed his lips to mine.

Heat built in the base of my stomach, blooming like a forgotten flower, flaring with heat, radiating down into my hips, thighs, traveling into the ground beneath me as his earth magic thrummed its song into my body.

Liam pulled away with a soft gasp as the crowd behind us burst into applause.

That was...

Interesting, I sent, more than a little flustered and wondering what things would be like later. When we were alone. And this dress and his tux weren't between us.

Growl.

No time for such carnal thoughts, at least, not yet. We were swarmed by our loved ones as we turned, Varity pronouncing the obvious.

"Coven Leader Hayle," she said, "and her mate, Gatekeeper Liam Hayle."

Oops. That little detail slipped my mind. But Liam didn't seem to mind, beaming as he bent to hug his mother.

Right, I'd forgotten Sonja was going to be here. But from the happiness on her face, the way she hugged me with enthusiasm, I knew Liam's influence had to still be in full action.

Otherwise, I was sure this wedding would never have happened. She'd have done her very best to make sure Liam didn't make it to the altar. And while I was a little weird with the whole working magic on his own mother thing, the alternative was me single and still looking, or dealing with a whacked-out mother-in-law.

And I didn't like either alternative, thanks.

I'm not sure if Liam laid on a bit more of his power, but she vanished and didn't bug me the rest of the reception. Or maybe it was just the fact I was then engulfed in hug after embrace after sloppy kiss of congratulations, depending on the person or animal delivering the message.

I'm sure the food was delicious, though I had no time to taste much of it. I spent the majority of the next several hours talking, dancing, being told I was beautiful and, best of all, just being with the people I cared about most in the world.

Uncle Frank's dance was fun, mostly because he teased me the entire time while Sunny glared at him and shook her head, probably knowing he planned to embarrass me.

I won't repeat what he said. I can hardly bring myself to rethink the conversation.

Blush. Ing.

Apollo's crudely hilarious dance with me ended abruptly as his sister led him away with an angry scowl. I seemed to recall this happening at the last wedding, too.

Some things never changed.

Dad's happiness for me when we took a turn was tempered only by the sad looks he cast at Mom. I wanted to comfort him, but there really wasn't anything to say.

To my surprise, I turned from my father and found myself scooped into the arms of Piers Southway. He spun me out onto the grass, long, blonde hair hanging over his shoulder, the familiar scent of coffee and mint making me smile as his sorcery butted heads with mine in greeting.

"Gorgeous," he murmured, bending to kiss my cheek. "He's a lucky sod and I'll be forever in the throes of envy."

I laughed, twirling as he turned me around. "I guess this means you'll have to find someone else to rescue you from now on," I said.

Piers stopped, pressing my hand to his heart in mock despair. "Alas," he said. "What will I ever do without you?"

I looked over to find Liam watching us, a curious look on his face. And blew him a kiss.

His smile returned as he caught it and settled it over his heart.

"Oh, for goodness sakes," Piers scowled, with humor in his eyes. "That's disgusting."

I stopped dancing as the music ended and patted his cheek. "Thank you for coming," I said. Paused. "You're just here for the wedding?"

He kissed me softly on the lips and I let him, the tingle I remembered no longer stirring me the way it used to as the power between Liam and I throbbed softly against the sorcerer's caress. "Don't go looking for trouble, sweetness," he said. "It's your wedding day."

Bratski.

And yet, was that a gleam of intent in his eyes? What was Piers up to as he left me, went to bend his head in close conversation with Varity?

Hmmm…

I felt Liam reach for me, turned again, train of worry broken, beaming, full of joy. And for a long, seemingly endless moment, it was he and I and the magic singing between us.

Congratulations, Ameline's mental voice broke through my happiness and slapped my temper so hard my demon howled in fury. *For saddling yourself with further baggage.* She laughed coldly. *Well done.*

I cut her off, Liam's power thrumming with concern as I shook my head, mood ruined.

The bitch.

Fighting for the return of my good humor, I stood there and watched the family gather around Liam. The twins hugged him, their wrinkled apple faces turned up as Estelle and Esther, in matching pink mother-of-the-bride outfits so classic I knew they'd had them for decades, kept control of him by their linked arms through his. I could feel the outpour of love from the coven. They adored Liam, were thrilled with my choice. With the fact I'd finally gotten hitched, more likely.

Still, it made me feel instantly better, knowing things worked out so well.

Ameline could bite me.

Enough already. I strode across the lawn to Liam's side, the gathered partygoers separating to allow me through. I came to a halt a few feet from him, cocking one hip to the side, right hand on my waist, left hand extended. The sparkling diamond caught the light as I wiggled my fingers at my new husband.

"Time to go," I said, voice unintentionally deep.

Hormones. Seriously.

Liam flushed as the crowd laughed, Uncle Frank slapping him on the back, whispering something in Liam's ear as he flushed even redder.

But he grinned when he came to me, took my hand, our power connecting with growing strength as he hooked his arm around my waist and pulled me to him, bending me back as he kissed me.

So freaking romantic. Sheesh.

When we straightened, our family cheered as I waved, tore the veil open and dragged him through it after me.

chapter five

The Sidhe cavern welcomed us with a sigh of power, embracing me as though understanding we were now one, Liam and I. It was odd to be suddenly in the cool dimness, a vast change from the chattering noise and laughter of the back yard.

Liam didn't seem to notice, sweeping me into his arms, carrying me across the threshold of his room, setting me gently down on the bed before closing the door. I felt the wards part, the touch of Galleytrot's power as he arrived, settling in to guard us. We'd already discussed with him our desire to have our first night alone, without interruption.

I knew the big hound would do everything he could to give us our privacy.

Liam stood looking at me, wonder and a hint of

shyness in his face.

Seriously? I stood, went to him as he ran his fingers through his hair, blushing again.

"I love you, Syd." His hands shook as he stroked the veil back from my shoulders.

"Silly," I said. "I love you, too." I slid my hands under his jacket, slipped it from his shoulders, ignoring it when it hit the floor with a soft whisper. His tie went next, vest buttons popping open under my fingers as I made slow but steady progress.

His hazel eyes flared green as he waited, patient and trembling, for me to discard the vest, working on the collar of his shirt. Three buttons and I leaned in, drawing a deep breath of him, loving the scent of his fabric softener, so familiar, and the rich, deep scent of fresh turned earth before finishing the job.

Liam shivered as my fingers traced down the center of his broad chest, over his hard stomach, tracing around his belly button. Paused at the top of his pants.

Grinned a wicked little grin.

He groaned, lifting me in the air, Sidhe power engulfing me with the surging power of a spring night, the wildness of a sudden thunderstorm pouring through my veins.

Heating the warm place at the pit of my stomach as he pressed his need against me.

I answered with a growl of passion I didn't expect.

My dress was simple to remove. I made sure of that.

His pants were no less problematic.

And then, I didn't have to think about anything anymore, anticipation paling in comparison to the feel of his skin on mine.

Something soft touched the end of my nose. I swatted at it, only to have it brush me again. My eyes cracked open, crankiness evaporating at the sight of Liam's eyes, so full of love, gazing into mine.

His finger hovered over my face, the tickling culprit. "Sorry," he said, voice thick. "I didn't want to wake you. But I couldn't stand it."

I giggled and burrowed into his chest, snuggling deeper in the big bed canopied by the leaves above. His long, strong body seemed to absorb me, making us one person as the fire inside, kindled the night before, blew awake from embers and roared to life again.

"Want some breakfast?" He kissed my forehead.

"Since you offered," I growled. And bit him.

It was several more hours before, showered and dressed, we emerged from his room in search of food and fresh air. Though I would have happily spent the whole day breathing him in. It would have been even better to run off somewhere for a week or so and just be the two of us.

We both knew that would never happen. Not with our responsibilities weighing us down.

Maybe, at some point, we'd be able to wrangle a day or two as a honeymoon, but, for now, I was just happy to know he'd be sleeping in the same bed with me every night.

Galleytrot rose from his place at the entry, silent, but his power emanating happiness. I hugged the big hound's head, stroking his ears, before standing and stretching, feeling amazing all of a sudden. Not a bit tired and, in fact, more energized than I'd ever felt.

My growling stomach made Liam laugh as he kissed me gently, spark of magic passing between us, before he bent and lifted a box into his arms.

"Time to go home," he said with a sweet smile.

Home. Right.

Though not exactly accurate. As I tore open the veil, I wondered how well our agreed upon arrangement would work out. Knowing how important the Sidhe cavern was, we worked out a schedule of back and forth—a night at the house, a night here—so we could keep an eye on everything. While it seemed a good idea when we talked it out, I wasn't so sure now.

And not in the way I thought I'd feel, either. The quiet and solitude of the cavern was such a nice change from the busyness of the house, I wondered how much time we'd actually spend at Liam's.

If I had my way? A lot.

Ahbi hugged me, hugged a startled Liam, as she deposited us in the kitchen at home. He smiled in happy surprise as she closed the veil behind us, cheeks pink.

"I didn't think she liked me," he said, oh so softly it almost broke my heart.

"She adores you," I said, hugging him. "Everyone does."

Well. Not everyone.

Sigh.

The house felt quiet. Nothing fell apart, no panic gripped the air. Awesome. Though it wasn't long before Shenka emerged from the basement, a huge smile on her face.

"Hungry, you two?" She went right to the fridge as I laughed and went to her, hugged her before she could start to cook.

"You don't have to take care of us," I said. "We're fine making our own lunch." Or supper. What the hell time was it, anyway?

Shenka rolled her eyes. "Seriously?" She turned away to start assembling our meal. "I've tasted your cooking, Syd. Your mother's lack of culinary skills runs in the family."

Smartass second.

Charlotte came downstairs, all bouncy and happy, hugging us both in turn before helping Shenka make our late lunch. We'd lost most of the day in bed, but I was okay with that. Was actually considering trotting off upstairs when dinner was done to see how much more time we could lose track of when Sassafras leaped up onto the table and fixed me with his amber eyes.

"Well," he said, "nice of you two to show up."

I swatted at him while Liam choked on his glass of water, blushing all over again. The poor guy was going to burst a few blood vessels at this rate.

"Mind your own business, cat," I said. "The world didn't blow up or anything, so we're good."

He snorted over the saucer of milk Shenka set before him.

"There's that," he said.

Charlotte handed me a plate of casserole, Shenka depositing a large loaf of garlic bread in the center of the table before disappearing down the hall with a tray. Gone to deliver some dinner to Gram, I could only guess. My heart clenched as I stared down at my food, only lifting my eyes when I felt Liam's distress.

I'm sorry about Ethpeal, he sent.

It's not your fault, I sent with a hug of magic.

Maybe not, he sent. *But still.*

Yeah. I knew what he meant.

I'd barely taken a bite when the air beside me flared with blue power and Mom appeared. Her smile and hug were tempered with a touch of anxiety. I knew she was genuinely happy to be here, but I also understood she had an ulterior motive.

"Liam." She kissed him gently before hugging Charlotte, stroking Sassy's fur and then sinking into her own chair, eyes locked on mine. "Did you have a nice night, kids?"

I laughed, spitting out some food as Liam coughed with his ears on fire.

Mom patted his back, evil smile fading as she turned to me again. "I'm happy to hear it," she said. "But I'm afraid I'm here to break up the party for the time being."

I perked, not really worried since the feeling from her wasn't so much anxious, I realized, but impatient.

"What's up?" I took a drink from my water glass as Shenka returned, smiling at Mom who waved to my second before speaking.

"Femke Svensson has invited you to visit," she said. "Officially."

That could only mean one thing. "Pannera?" Had to be. Was there finally movement on the vampire queen?

"The invitation only said you were to come to Oxford at your convenience," Mom said. "But I had the distinct impression, from the irritation in her message, she's finally had enough of the undead leader's stalling."

Wicked. Relief poured through me at the thought of finally freeing Sebastian and his blood clan from the not-so-tender mercies of Celeste Oberman. And the

38

Brotherhood.

Mom's regretful smile for Liam paired with a soft pat to his hand. "I'm sorry, dear," she said. "Syd has to work."

He shook his head, a crooked smile on his face. "Why am I not surprised?"

My grin was backed by a magical hug as I surged to my feet, the old need to act turned into the freedom to do just that.

My favorite.

CHAPTER SIX

Why did I think I'd be traveling alone? The moment I stepped back from kissing Liam goodbye, Charlotte took her place at my side, expression flat and no-nonsense.

I rolled my eyes at her and took my werefriend's hand. "Yes, Mom," I said.

My actual mother laughed as Charlotte's expression softened into a grin. "You two be good now," she said. "Play nice with the nasty vampire lady."

We'd see.

The veil parted before me, Charlotte right at my side as Ahbi scooped us up and carried us, in a pair of heartbeats, across the Atlantic. I stepped out of the rubbery membrane and into a large office to the startled but welcoming power of the European Council Leader.

She stood from behind her desk, coming around to take my hand, shaking first mine and then Charlotte's.

"Syd," Femke said, tall, lean body towering over me, faint Scandinavian accent coloring her English, "that was fast. I just spoke to your mother."

I shrugged and sat in one of the velvet-upholstered chairs, eyes drifting to the window and the nighttime view of Oxford University lit in cold, white lights. Charlotte stood behind me in her old place as though to remind me why she was here. "I've been waiting a long time for this little problem to go away," I said. "Thanks for the invite."

Femke sat back, hands folded in front of her, smiling at me. It was the first time I speculated as to her age, her grin making her look far younger than I first thought. No matter what kind of horrors Margaret Applegate, the old Leader, visited on her people while under control of the Brotherhood, this last act, choosing Femke as her successor, made up for it one hundred fold. I liked everything about the progressive witch, including the fact she didn't seem to hold to formality.

"Congratulations, by the way," she said. "How was the wedding?"

"Fun." I fiddled with my rings. "At least the Council is happy at last."

She snorted. "Stupid law, really. And your situation is making me think maybe we should do something about it."

Now she told me. "A bit late, aren't you?"

Femke laughed. "What, you wanted things to go easy

41

for you for once?" We'd had a few talks over the last two weeks, and she'd been more than sympathetic about the troubles I'd lived through. "Surely, you jest. Where's the fun in that?"

"Don't get me started," I said. "Seriously. Witch laws are stupid generally."

She snorted. "I've been reviewing some of the more abstract of them lately," she said. "You have no idea."

And didn't want to. "Just be a good leader and fix them, would you?"

Femke's pale blue eyes sparkled in the light from the low-hanging chandelier dominating the domed ceiling of her office. "Doing my best. Starting with your vampire friends."

Ah. I was right then.

"Tell me you're finally going to let me kick Pannera's ass?" Couldn't. Freaking. Wait. I sat forward, hands on my bouncing knees, trying to ignore the full-sized portrait of an old, cranky-looking witch hanging over Femke's head. Like she was judging me for my eagerness.

Femke shook her head, but not in denial. "I've tried everything," she said, looking out into the English nighttime sky, the last sliver of the dying moon's light reflecting back through the glass. "And I've allowed her every opportunity to create a dialogue. But she refuses to even permit me inside her castle. And threats from Enforcers, my last resort, left me empty handed."

Femke's gaze returned to mine. "How can you stand it?"

"I don't." I leaned forward and tapped her desk with two fingers. "Mind if I try knocking on her door?"

Femke bobbed a nod, long, blonde hair in a tight ponytail swinging as she did. "Have some fun for me, too, will you?" She stood, offered her hand. "Maji Sydlynn Hayle," she said in a formal voice, power behind it as her Council magic swelled and welcomed me through her touch. "I would ask that you attend to this matter for me and, in this and all things, I offer you the trust of the European Council you will act in the best interests of all witches and magic folk."

The Council magic embraced me, flared and set me free.

Holy. "You realize you just cut me loose from law in your territory." Just to make things clear.

Femke didn't smile, just kept her gaze steady. "We need you, Syd," she said. "You've proven that time and again. And now that I've come to know you better, I can't bring myself to limit you or the actions I know are necessary to the safety of my covens."

Whoa.

"I won't betray that trust," I said, choking up a little. "Ever."

She smiled finally, came around her desk to hug me. "Syd," she said. "I wouldn't have offered if I thought any different." Femke's strong hands gripped my arms.

"While I don't envy your path in life, I do envy your sense of loyalty and justice. I can only hope to, one day, be half as committed to the safety of our plane as you are."

Okay, enough with the supernatural waterworks.

I stepped back, flushed and a little breathless, feeling I didn't deserve so much faith, but knowing, now it was in my possession, I couldn't fail.

I just couldn't.

"Council Leader Svensson," I saluted her with hand to my heart, "thank you."

Charlotte and I returned to the veil as Femke waved, my pulse running too fast, struggling with what she'd said.

So much pressure. But I was used to that, wasn't I?

My werefriend's surprise when the veil parted and we stepped out into the main foyer of the palace in Ukraine almost made me laugh. Would have, if I wasn't still freaked out by the whole faith thing with Femke.

She met my eyes, one brow cocked in curiosity.

"I thought it might be a good idea to warn your grandfather," I said as I turned and headed for the throne room. "Considering the old animosity between werewolves and vampires, it might be smart for him to know all hell might be breaking loose shortly."

Charlotte nodded as she kept pace with me. "Thoughtful of you," she said.

"I'm nice like that." I grinned at her as we strode past the bowing wereguards and across the polished marble floor to where Oleksander sat on his throne, talking to a tall, handsome someone in a gray longcoat.

Piers turned with a smile, offering his hand as I approached, kissing my cheek gently. But his eyes avoided mine after our initial contact and I couldn't help but wonder what he was up to.

Oleksander didn't give me the opportunity to grill my suddenly shy friend. The giant werewolf swept Piers out of the way, embracing me with a hearty laugh. My feet left the floor as the enthusiastic king of the werewolves hugged me in a giant, rib-cracking squeeze before setting me on my feet again.

I gasped for breath as Charlotte scowled at her grandfather.

"*Didus*," she said, voice heavy with disappointment.

He kissed her soundly before rubbing his hands together. "Sydlynn," he said. "Please accept the congratulations of the werewolf nation on your marriage."

I smiled and nodded as I got my wind back. "Thanks," I said.

"You enjoyed our gift?" He looked at Charlotte with clear expectation as I wracked my brain for what he had sent us. The gift unwrapping happened a few days ago in a flurry of other people standing around watching me decimate wrapping paper while overwhelmed with the need to be anywhere but there at that moment.

Which meant I already forgot what Liam and I received. Though I was sure I saw Shenka scrawling things in a notebook, hadn't I? Which meant thank you cards would have to go out.

Yikes.

I'd take worldwide apocalypse any day.

"She loved the carvings, *Didus*," Charlotte said, saving my ass, eyes meeting mine as her wolf appeared in them. She didn't have to be that amused by my clear lack of memory retention. Yup. She knew I forgot.

But her prompt raised the memory and, with a quickly suppressed wince, I tried a smile.

"Lovely," I said, wondering where the hell we were going to put the giant wooden scene of a pack of wolves running under moonlight. Oleksander's version of a velvet Elvis would probably end up stored in the basement.

"Thank you so much," I said, struggling for something nice to say. "It's lovely."

Weak. Oh, so weak. But Oleksander beamed, thick silver beard bristling in his happiness, so I guess I did okay.

"Now that your wedding is over," he said, "perhaps my Sharlotta will learn from your example and finally be convinced to choose her own mate." His brows pulled down over his forehead as he fixed her with his wolf eyes.

I felt her tense beside me, glanced over to see her

tight frown flicker for a heartbeat before her stoic expression returned.

"Yes, *Didus*," she said without a hint of agreement.

He gusted a sigh while my heart hurt for her.

And blurted my opinion out of turn. Because, I had this thing with my mouth and my brain and no filter.

What else was new?

"Your majesty," I said, despite being on first name terms with the big werewolf. "Might I make a suggestion?"

He nodded quickly, almost eager for my input.

I just wasn't sure he'd like it as much as he seemed to think he would.

"Charlotte is young," I said. "And while witch law insisted I marry, your culture doesn't have such restrictions." I guessed. Turned to my friend, felt her tension easing, knew I hit a bull's eye. "Considering how very little time you've all had to adjust to being free, rushing into a marriage at this point would, I believe, take away Charlotte's most valuable discovery: her freedom."

Oleksander's frown told me he wanted to argue, but I rushed on before he could.

"There is plenty of time," I said. "And the perfect match for her, for your race, isn't something to be chosen lightly." I shrugged, forcing casual into a situation I knew could be volatile if I took a wrong turn. "Since there are a variety of races with magic abilities Charlotte can now choose from, you need to decide," I winked at her, "as a family," like she'd let that happen, "if keeping your werewolf blood pure is the right decision or would you be better served bringing in other magicks to bolster your power."

Could have gone either way. I did my best to stand there when I was done and not react as a mixture of expressions passed over Oleksander's face.

And then, at last, he nodded, blowing out a gust of air, mustache shivering from it. "You speak wisely," he said as the tension in my stomach unwound. "But I worry for our race. For our family." Oleksander focused on Charlotte. "I am old. And would like to step down for younger blood to wear the crown. Such an idea that we could mate with other races has crossed my mind. And I'm not certain if I, as hide-bound as I have become, am the right one to adapt to such possibilities." He hooked both thumbs in his wide belt, chin dropping to his chest. "My Sharlotta is the last of my direct line and, as my heir, needs some of her own, whether they be pure born werewolves or a hybrid of our race and another."

I could tell it troubled him. Felt the stirring of unhappiness from the gathered pack who watched and listened.

"Again," I said, "you've been free such a short time, you've had almost no opportunity to even decide the best path for your people. How then, great king, can you ask your granddaughter and heir to rush a decision that could carry massive repercussions for the future of the werewolf nation?"

Oh boy, was I getting good at this political speak stuff. Even I felt chuffed by how I'd wrangled my argument into a nice, neat package.

Oleksander's chin sank lower.

Time to seal the deal.

"Have faith in her," I said, taking Charlotte's hand. She squeezed gently back. "You've done very well raising her. And protecting your people, as far as you were able. Now is the time for your race to understand freedom is the most important gift you possess." I smiled, hugging Charlotte. "Including the freedom to wait if that's what works for you."

Oleksander nodded heavily, head rising at last. "Very well," he said. Smiled at his granddaughter. "I will not push you further, my sweet Sharlotta," he said. "The choice will be yours."

She twitched before lunging forward to hug her grandfather.

They whispered together a moment in Ukrainian as Piers shook his head at me, a little smile on his face.

Well, aren't you Miss Sunshine, he sent. *Spreading joy wherever you go.*

That's me, I sent with a grin. *Why, you need some, poor sorcerer boy?*

His power turned lecherous, tinted with good humor. *Depends on what you're spreading*, he sent.

Flirtasaurus.

Didn't stop me from remembering his initial reaction to my arrival though.

Nice try on the evade and distract, I sent. *What are you up to?*

Me? His mental voice laughed. *I think you're imagining things, Coven Leader.*

That wasn't a "nothing", I sent.

Piers cut me off with a smirk.

Oh no, he did *not*. If he was planning on stirring up some trouble I'd likely have to clean up after him—considering our previous adventures when he defied his mother in an attempt to free the weres from the Black Souls before teaming up with me against Vasyl at conclave—I'd pin him to the ground and beat him senseless.

I didn't get to press him further. Oleksander and Charlotte finished talking, both turning to me as Charlotte hooked her arm through his.

"Sydlynn has news," she said.

Right. It only took a moment to fill in the werewolf king on my plan to go against Pannera. Piers frowned thoughtfully, his expression only reaching my peripheral vision, but enough to make me nervous.

Oleksander stiffened when I was through speaking,

anger rippling around him. "My people are at your service, maji," he said.

"That won't be necessary," I said, chuckling internally at the crazy honor and dedication of the werewolf race. Maybe Charlotte would be better off marrying outside her people. Bring them some perspective already. "But thank you. I just wanted you to know I'm about to kick the hornet's nest."

Charlotte bowed to her grandfather. "I'd like to accompany Sydlynn," she said.

He nodded immediately. "Go with our blessing," he said. "And serve with honor."

Sigh. Nipping that one in the bud right freaking now.

"No," I said. "Not serve. Never serve again."

His smile was so boyish I almost laughed.

"You honor us." Oleksander kissed both of my cheeks before letting us go. "Keep us informed."

I waved, walked away, Charlotte beside me. Heard Piers say a hasty farewell to Oleksander before the thudding sound of his fast feet caught up.

Why wasn't I surprised? I'd purposely walked away from him, hoping he'd be unable to resist the lure of adventure and, maybe in his haste to find out what I had planned, would give up his own.

Because the moment I met his gray eyes, I knew for certain he had bigger things in mind. Things with which he likely wanted my help.

"I'd like to join you," he said.

Of course he would.

"Just make sure you stay out of trouble," I said, poking him with magic. "I don't have time to save your butt." Paused. "Now or later, you hear me?"

His sorcery bumped mine. "We'll see who does the saving."

Snort.

I felt Ahbi's welcome as we stepped into the veil, Piers holding my left hand, fingers pressing my rings into my skin. I could have pushed him harder, and planned to, but right now Sebastian was my focus.

I couldn't wait to see my vampire friend again.

Thank you, Charlotte sent as we stepped out on the other side, into a familiar stone hall graced with tall, lifelike portraits of long-dead Wilhelms. *You didn't have to speak for me.*

I did. I let Piers go but kept my hold on her, feeling the power of her magic even stronger than before. *You deserve the right to choose your own path, Charlotte.*

I really should marry, she sent. *I have a duty to my people.* I looked up as Sunny approached, a smile on her face. But I turned to Charlotte, instead, and pressed my forehead to hers.

Listen to me, I sent. *You are Charlotte Girard, weregirl, before you are Princess Sharlotta Moreau, heir to the werenation. Don't ever forget that.*

She shivered. *You didn't have that choice.*

I know, I sent back. *Why do you think your freedom is so important to me?*

I felt Sunny waiting for us, took a last moment to hug Charlotte with power and my arms, before turning to the smiling vampire queen.

"Hi, Sunny," I said. "Feel like storming Castle Sthol?"

The sudden surge of spirit magic and the nasty smile on the gorgeous vampire's face were all the answer I needed.

chapter seven

I walked the length of the throne room at Castle Wilhelm, smiling at the welcoming vampires who nodded to me as we passed. Not the greeting I had initially, back when Batsheva Moromond led the blood clan, when the Brotherhood's taint controlled and manipulated the vampires. It was a nice change, the friendly greetings, compared to "We hate you forever, Sydlynn Hayle."

Well, most of the vampires welcomed me. With one clear and furious exception. Piotr Wilhelm used to keep his distance, his twisted heart still aimed right at my destruction. For some reason beyond any understanding, he blamed me for the death of Yvette, his beloved queen. Personally, any ruler who fell to the likes of Batsheva Moromond got what she deserved.

This time was different, for the first time. His go-to tattletale recipient was gone, since Council Leader

Margaret Applegate's retreat from the leadership and her ties to the Brotherhood ended with conclave. Piotr's frustration shone clear on his face as he took a step forward, past his queen.

Into my space.

"You're not welcome here," he snarled, showing fang.

"Really feeling the love, Pete," I said. Waved my hand in front of my face. "You might want to do something about your breath, old boy. Rank."

Sunny was at his side a snapping instant later, one hand around his throat, claws extended, indenting his pale skin.

"You go too far," she hissed. "And have been warned in the past."

He didn't look as scared as he should have. "Then kill me, my queen," he said. "Take my life. Because I will never welcome this thing," he flipped one hand at me, lace cuff bouncing around his smooth flesh, "here."

I didn't come here to witness a vampire fight. Or to relive my own draining, thanks. Still had the odd nightmare about Batsheva's face and all those teeth and mouths on me.

Shudder.

I saw Sunny's hesitation and wondered. Worried for a moment. Not that I thought violence was the answer to everything—some things, sure—but if Sunny wasn't strong enough to control her blood clan, if a challenge like this one went unanswered, there could be major problems in undead land.

Problems I didn't need.

"Your majesty," I said. "If you wouldn't mind? I hate to intrude on vampire law, but I'm the one he insulted. Might I ask permission to deal with him personally? Save you the trouble of getting blood on your beautiful dress." Pink tonight. Lovely, really.

Would be a shame.

Her eyes lit with agreement as she leaned closer and whispered in Piotr's ear. "You'd better hope the maji is more understanding than I am," she hissed. "And that she spares you. Because you have had your last warning. Disobey me again, and your blood is mine."

He flinched. Okay, so he was scared. Staggered as Sunny gave him a solid shove toward me. Only to impact against my shields and bounce away with a howl of pain as the rippling magic seared him with demon fire.

"Thank you, most gracious queen," I said, bowing to her. Turned to Piotr. "You hurt my feelings," I said. "I don't like meanies."

He didn't say anything, staring at me with a mix of loathing and concern.

"What do you think, Your Highness?" I turned to Charlotte who watched him with her wolf in her eyes, body loose and ready for a fight. "Dismemberment? And then, disembowelment, I'm thinking." I turned to her with a bright smile. "I'll let you eat his heart."

She didn't crack a smile. "Most kind of you, maji," she growled.

I turned back to Piotr, frowning as I tapped my chin with one finger. "Hmmm. Then again, he'd probably poison you," I said. Sighed and threw my hands in the air. "I guess I'll just have to use fire."

"The cleanest method, maji," Charlotte said.

"It is," I said. "And would save poor Sunny having to have her floor scrubbed." My vampire friend's lips tightened as Uncle Frank coughed behind one hand. Nice to know they were enjoying themselves.

Okay, fine. They weren't the only ones.

Piotr swayed where he stood, head dropping. "Forgive me, maji," he said. So softly I barely heard him.

Tipped my head to the side, fingers by my ear. "Sorry, what was that, Pete?"

I saw his lips curl, fangs appearing again as his hands fisted at his side. But he looked up and met my eyes.

"My apologies," he said. "For my rudeness."

"Oh," I said, smiling at Charlotte, turning to beam at the watching vampires. "He's sorry. So that's all right then, isn't it?" I let my own vampire out as I lunged the next moment, one hand at his throat as Sunny had done, the other over his chest, all five fingers pressing into the soft velvet of his frock coat. "You challenge me again," I said, "and what Sunny plans to do to you will feel like a picnic in the park. Because she can only kill you once."

White fire flared in his eyes, but he nodded.

I released him, dusted my hands together. And walked away from him.

Thank you, Sunny sent.

Um-hum. I followed her to the back of the throne room without saying anything further. We sat in the private cubby behind the thrones, Uncle Frank perched next to Sunny as Charlotte and Piers took seats on either side of me. I spotted Piotr still watching, but had no worries about him anymore.

The asshat little traitor was scared of me at last. And without Sunny's support, with no one to watch his back, he'd put himself into the final line of fire. It made me wonder, though, if his network of tattletaling had fallen on hard times or if he still, somehow, had a connection to the Brotherhood.

No way. Not with the repressed fury in him, the way he felt so helpless in his rage. Piotr was on his own, had made his coffin and now had to lurk in it alone.

Boo freaking hoo.

"You really need to do something about him," I said as I watched him turn and leave the throne room, knowing it was true, ultimately. That kind of animosity wouldn't just sit lightly. He might be out of power now, but who knew what darkness he'd sell his soul to in the state he was in? "I wouldn't be surprised Piotr will go looking for a way to interact directly with the Brotherhood."

Sunny nodded slowly. The last time I'd called her on him, she'd clearly sent a message my interference wasn't welcome, and fair enough. But this time she'd allowed me in, gave me the right to present an opinion by offering him to me, so I didn't feel like I was out of bounds on the topic anymore.

"I like to keep him close," she said. "Just in case I discover a way to use him against those who hold his reins."

I could understand that, but still. The Brotherhood were ahead of us at every corner. And allowing Piotr access to Sunny and Uncle Frank made me incredibly nervous. "I just want to remind you about Celeste and Mom's decision to keep her around," I said, keeping my tone mild. "And how well that little plan worked out."

Sunny's grimace wasn't aimed at me. "Noted," she said. "Now, tell me about how we're going to destroy Pannera and drain her whole clan to the dregs."

Vicious. I grinned and shrugged, letting Piotr be Sunny's problem. "Femke's a little sick of being ignored," I said. "Asked me to drop by and see what Pannera's problem is." I folded my hands in my lap, giggling inside at the excitement of action—such an adrenaline junkie— while feigning casual nonchalance. "Thought you might like to come along for the ride."

Sunny rose to her feet, curtsying with a grace only the undead could master.

"I'm at your service, maji," she said with a truly terrible twinkle in her eye.

I loved Sunny so much.

In the end, though he grumbled and complained, we left Uncle Frank behind.

"Just in case this goes badly," Sunny said to him, gripping his hands in hers, earnest love passing between them, so powerful I felt it from steps away. "I need to know you are here, with our blood clan."

How many times had I left others to protect my family in similar circumstances? My heart hurt for both of them, though I knew this would end badly for one person and one person only. No matter what it took, Pannera was going down and I refused to let her take anyone else with her.

"I assume I'm still invited?" Piers watched me with hooded eyes as Sunny joined us. "As an objective observer, naturally."

I took his hand again as Sunny gripped my free one, Charlotte's hand on my shoulder. "Naturally. Besides, I want to keep my eyes on you for now. And have a talk later about what it is you have up your long, gray sleeves."

He didn't comment. Or argue.

Which meant I wasn't going to like it even a little bit. The veil opened and I honestly half-expected a horde of

European Enforcers to appear, to stop me from acting, Margaret Applegate at their head, snapping with power, the taint of the Brotherhood firmly holding her in thrall. But we stepped unfettered through the gap, Ahbi carrying us safely through the veil, and out the other side.

Not exactly in the middle of the Sthol throne room as I'd planned. In fact, the breeze cutting across the mountain pass at the gate was as familiar as the sight of the group of vampires snarling and blocking our path.

Expecting us. So Piotr still had his contacts here. Why was I not surprised?

It didn't matter. The fact I was stopped here, outside the castle, drove my worry up a notch. I shouldn't have had restrictions, not with my maji power in full force. And yet, something kept me from entering, a power at once familiar and not. But whoever it was, that power swelled by the moment, filling with the darkness of sorcery and holding me at bay with the very taint keeping Pannera in thrall.

I had to get in there. Now.

I released my friends, feeling Sunny swell and change as her true form emerged, shuddering inwardly at the glimpse of her out of the corner of my eye, all teeth and fangs and transparent skin. Charlotte half-changed behind me, the push of her wolf against my back even as the black emptiness of Piers's power flowed outward, pushing up against my sorcery.

I didn't plan on needing them, but it was nice to have the backup.

"Evening," I said to the snarling vampires in full-blown defense mode, as spooky as any Hollywood version, but no match for me. "I'm here to see your queen." My maji power rose in a spinning column of iridescence, surrounding me in a sparkling tornado of creation power.

They stared, looked around in fear as they realized I wasn't taking no for an answer.

"Knock, knock," I said. And hit them full-force with the strength of my magic.

I think they landed somewhere in Africa. I'd have to check with Ife Maalouf, the Council Leader for that territory, and find out for sure.

Meanwhile, the doors to the castle stood undefended. And opened with a thundering bang as my maji energy made short work of the magic holding them closed.

I turned to Sunny who shrank back to her stunningness and bowed a little. "After you, Your Majesty," I said.

She curtsied in response. "Why, thank you," she said before strolling inside.

Piers grinned at me. "You have the most fun," he said.

I laughed as Charlotte gave me a gentle push between the shoulder blades to get me moving.

Was it wrong I agreed with him?

The moment I passed through the front gate, I felt Pannera's power retreat from me, howling in madness, paired with that familiar power. So familiar, masked in emptiness, humming with blue.

Enforcer?

What the hell was going on?

No way was I letting her escape, my magic engulfing the castle as I ripped at the veil, my friends around me, now able to ride right to the vampire queen.

Emerged in a throne room so similar to Sunny's I almost did a double take.

Didn't have time.

Not when I finally saw the reason for the vampire queen's retreat, the source of the magic I knew and didn't, hovering over the fallen undead leader, drawing out a pool of black as it siphoned from all the vampires in the room.

The taint. Pulled free and devoured.

By Ameline Benoit.

Pannera collapsed the rest of the way as the last of the Brotherhood's black power left her and slammed into my nemesis. Ameline smiled at me, wiping delicately at her mouth, touched with blood. It was clear from the red marks on Pannera's neck Ameline had bitten her to start the transfer.

I shuddered with disgust, grateful I didn't need to

feed that way in order to free Sunny.

"The bitch is liberated," Ameline said. "You're welcome." I lashed out to capture her, knowing now how close she was to being complete maji, fear surging even as blue power flared, the Enforcer magic I'd felt, no longer shielded from my touch, the same power she'd stolen from my grandmother reaching back for me before Ameline vanished.

Her laughter echoing in my head as she went.

chapter eight

Sunny went right to her rival, lifting the fallen queen into her arms with a tenderness I didn't expect. The Sthol Family Blood Clan moaned around the room, seemingly worse affected by the draining than the Wilhelm's had been. Piles of fallen vampires lay everywhere, tangled among themselves as though they'd clung to each other for support prior to collapsing.

They've been under the influence of the taint far longer, Sunny sent. *And, from the feeling of them, being the main focus since you freed my family hasn't served them well.*

I crouched next to Pannera as Charlotte and Piers paced around the room, assisting the vampires. The queen's eyes fluttered open, her face a sunken mummy mask, though not completely drained. But her clear gray eyes, almost colorless in shock, locked on mine, as full of life as they had ever been. She grasped my hand with a withered hand, nails digging into my skin.

"What..." she trailed off. "What's happened?"

Sunny soothed her, feeding her energy even as the other vampire queen gulped it up. Her skin swelled, filled out a fraction while I augmented Sunny's aid with the power of the vampire essence inside me.

She is very badly hurt, my vampire sent. *Her spirit magic is damaged.* She showed me the crumbling edges of the queen's power, the way it sparked and died away as we tried to reinforce it.

At least she's free, I sent while Sunny helped her sit up.

Pannera's grasp tightened as she leaned against me. "Maji," she whispered. "Forgive my failings. The Brotherhood's control over me was almost complete."

I held her up with my body, still feeding her power though my vampire pulled away after only a little while, doing more harm than good. "Great Queen," I said, "I'm just happy to see you liberated."

Sure, she'd been a bitch to me when the Brotherhood controlled her. But she was a ruler long before they took her over and, I figured, I owed her that much courtesy for holding out as long as she did.

A handful of her people came forward, falling to their knees before her. She touched their faces, power sparking, though I saw and felt the toll her exchange took. Still, they smiled as their own magic was restored and, after their bond renewed, they gently lifted her and carried her to her throne.

While I sat there and gnawed my lower lip raw over the fact Ameline now had almost all the power she needed.

All but one.

I stood and turned to Pannera as she sagged in her throne. "Queen of the Sthol Blood Clan," I said. "I request a boon."

She nodded as her vampires came to huddle around her as though for comfort as much as connection. "Anything," she said, a wheezing sound ending on her exhale.

"Though not of your choosing," I said, "Celeste Oberman, the vampire who accompanied your enemy, Batsheva, once queen of Wilhelm and murderer of Yvette, has taken control of the Blood Clan DeWinter." A mouthful, but vampires loved formality and after my little spiel to Oleksander, it kind of came naturally. "She has captured and imprisoned Sebastian DeWinter and is starving the clan to weakness, as we speak."

Pannera may have been reduced, damaged, but her anger remained intact. She surged forward, show of power costing her—it had to—but almost seeming to make her stronger.

"Not for long," she snarled.

I approached, her vampires falling back from me in fear, and grasped her hand, not wanting her to waste energy in travel. "Allow me, Great Queen," I said.

Her thin fingers flexed around mine. "As you wish," she said. *Thank you*, her mind sent.

The veil welcomed her, Ahbi sensing how fragile she was through contact with me. She cradled us gently on our trip to Wilding Springs and just beyond, to the vampire mansion. There were no shields this time, no holding me back as Ahbi dropped us into the giant foyer in a flare of amber light.

Watch Meira, I sent as I left my grandmother's embrace.

Ahbi's power flared in rage and acknowledgment as she sealed the veil behind us.

At least my sister would be safe enough. For now.

Time to worry about Ameline once Sebastian was free and Celeste was dead.

I was really, really looking forward to both.

Once more with my faithful friends into battle. Charlotte on one side, Sunny on the other, Pannera gripped in the vampire queen's arms while Piers tagged along with a smirk of anticipation on his face, we strode through the large foyer of the vampire mansion ready to crush anyone in our way.

How delightful to find Celeste herself standing just inside the main hall on the right of the entry, staring at us in shock, hands trembling, magic flickering in pale ghosts of spirit.

She's weak, my vampire sent as my demon snuffled around the big undead woman. *When Ameline took the taint, Celeste lost her connection to the Brotherhood.*

Yes. My sorcery agreed, swelling outward as though sensing easy prey, its hunger grasping for the now violently shaking witch turned vampire.

Pannera's rage lashed outward, Celeste falling to her knees with a scream that echoed through the stone halls of the mansion. The damaged queen stumbled forward with Sunny on her arm, keeping her level, Pannera's clawed hands and protruding fangs glistening in the light.

"Traitor," she snarled, "defiler of the clan. I will drain you and dump your blood to be eaten by wild beasts."

A huge insult, Sunny sent.

I could only imagine. Blood was, after all, sacred to vampires. Having Celeste's discarded had to be the greatest of dishonors.

Celeste didn't seem to care all that much as she shuddered with pain, body pressed to the red carpet where she writhed under the power of her blood oath to her queen.

Shame, that.

I should have expected Pannera's strength to wane, but I was so focused on Celeste's suffering—yes, that made me a very bad person, I know—I failed to realize the old queen's power had left her in a rush before Celeste gasped and pushed herself to her feet in a desperate surge before spinning and running down the hall away from us.

Well, staggering. Charlotte growled beside me, loping after her in half-wolf form and I let her go.

She'd been a good girl. Deserved to have some fun.

Pannera collapsed, sinking to the stone floor as Sunny let her rest, even as vampires drifted closer, thin, ragged, their spirits almost broken as they looked at their queen.

Starving. Wretched.

Sebastian's first lieutenant, Anastasia came to the front, the normally stunning blonde vampire now emaciated, though she radiated hope around her hurt. "My queen," she wailed. "You've come to save us."

Excitement ran through the spirit power in the mansion, rippling with a murmur of need, tight and eager.

Pannera nodded slowly, though she could hardly hold her head up. "Your leader," she whispered. "The maji will free him."

I stepped forward, closing the distance to Anastasia. "Take me to Sebastian," I said.

She led me at a rapid pace, Piers beside me, down the same corridor Celeste fled through. I reached for Charlotte, felt her still in pursuit, left her to it. No matter the outcome, there was nowhere Celeste could hide from me now.

One way or another, she'd be dead the moment I had time to track her down.

As long as Charlotte didn't beat me to it.

I descended into the vaults below the mansion, though not into the maji chamber, but the very one where Batsheva imprisoned the vampires during Mom's trial. Rows of coffins lined the cold, damp walls, the one at the far end the most elaborate, sealed tightly with spirit magic and a skim of black sorcery.

Just a hint remained behind, obviously not tied to the power Ameline siphoned free, independent, slowly devouring the soul inside to keep itself intact. Piers's power cracked the edges of it before I had a chance to do so, powdering the darkness into dust. My vampire's spirit magic sliced free the remaining shields as I stepped back.

"Open it."

Anastasia did so, reduced by her starvation. But her undead strength more than a match for the cover of Sebastian's coffin.

I held my breath, knew what to expect. Had seen it before, his remains, withered and mummified, only his stunning blue eyes alive and aware. This time, not even that remained to him, dull emptiness meeting me as I leaned in and looked down into his sunken face.

My hand touched his cheek, dry and flaking. Fear drove its needles of fire through me as I reached with my power, letting the vampire call to him.

Sebastian. I couldn't feel him at all. Was he gone? How could he be? Tears blurred my vision as I fought my grief, my failure. I'd left it too long, allowed the Brotherhood to destroy my friend, to drain him until there was nothing left.

One of my tears dripped onto his barren cheek, glistening softly on the gray parchment of his flesh. I reached deeper, my vampire seeking, but not alone. Demon joined her, Sidhe, family power blazing a trail to his soul even as the sorcery inside me blossomed in answer.

We will not let him go, they said together.

And my maji power rose, engulfing him in iridescence, calling to my friend, begging him to come back from the dead.

No, not dead. Not yet. He was there, after all. But so close to being lost I knew it was only moments, seconds, heartbeats before Sebastian DeWinter was no more.

And I couldn't let that happen.

My creation magic surrounded his spirit, fed it from the fount of all power. I felt him draw on me, in a sip at first, barely there, hardly noticeable. But his strength increased as he absorbed what I offered, soft draw now greedy gulps, desperate and hopeful in a place where hope didn't live anymore. He rose with me, returning, slowly first, then faster, powerful, in a rush as I gave him access to the power of creation.

Sebastian's roar of life echoed in the room as he surged up and out of his coffin. Fully restored. Body perfect, flawless, power flaring around him in sparks of every color. He landed on his feet, spinning to face me.

Strode the five steps it took to come to my side and grasped me in his arms.

Kissed me with passion so powerful I swooned.

I kid you not. I read about swooning in romance novels. Thought it was all a load of bunk and someone's romantic idea of what being kissed should feel like, but not real.

Um. Yeah.

Swoonaroonie.

His kiss lingered, finally broke as he leaned away, a smile on his delicious face.

"I owe you again, it seems," he said in a voice throbbing with emotion.

Throbbing was a bad choice of words. Married.

Remember you're married.

"You're welcome," I said. Well, tried to. Whispered, really. All breathless and stuff.

Yikes.

"Your queen is here," Piers said, sounding amused. I turned my head to glare at him, caught him tsking silently while he waggled his eyebrows at me.

So that's how this marriage is going to go, he sent. *Good to know.*

Creep. He'd pay for that.

Sebastian seized my hand and turned, striding away,

power still rippling in waves of color. He felt different, but there was no time to process. Not while he practically ran me up the stairs and down the hall, halting at the sight of Pannera still lying on the floor next to Sunny.

He finally let me go, rushed to his queen's side, bent on one knee.

She reached out and touched his cheek, smiling. "My dear Sebastian," she said. "I worried so."

I almost missed the shock in her eyes, I was just so happy he was okay.

But when Pannera's head turned, her blazing fury focused on me, I realized something was wrong after all.

"Maji," she hissed as Sebastian stood, amazement on his face. "Do you mind telling me why my vampire is no longer mine?" She jabbed a finger at me. "And why that vampire now feels like you?"

Oh boy.

CHAPTER NINE

I didn't really think she had the right to be so pissed at me, considering the state she'd been in the last little while. And I'd been on the way to rescue her, hadn't I? Not my fault Ameline beat me to it.

Sebastian stared at me with open adoration, making me all kinds of uncomfortable as he left his queen to come stand by my side. I could feel it then, now I'd lost my shaky, overly adrenalized moment of joy-joy. How he felt different, his power more like mine.

More like a maji.

A quick check from my vampire confirmed he was still undead, and yet...

"I'm sorry," I said, not really feeling it at all, to be totally honest. At least, for Pannera. But when I looked up at Sebastian, regret raised its ugly head. "I didn't mean to break your blood bond." I thought of Charlotte, spotted her loping back into view, shifting into full human form as she shook her head.

Right. Celeste. Managed to escape, it appeared. But watching my werefriend gave me an idea as Sebastian's new power crawled over mine, as though looking for a place to merge.

"I can try to fix it," I said. "Remake the bond?"

Pannera might have been damaged and unable to rise on her own, but her piercing eyes never left the tall, delicious DeWinter as he laughed out loud and hugged me.

"No," he said, eyes sparkling as his cheeks flushed. "Never again." How? He hadn't drunk any blood.

Where was the blush coming from?

Pannera's sharp voice snapped his name. "Sebastian! Return to my side at once!"

He was already turning toward the exit as though she hadn't spoken. I pulled him back by my hold on his hand, still stunned by the cheerful, almost boyish look on his face. I'd never seen him so glowing, more handsome than ever, a tiny shiver of desire quickly batted aside as I tried to focus.

On anything but the way he looked at me.

"Sebastian," I said. "Your blood clan. You'll just abandon them?"

His forehead pulled together, a quick nod bouncing his dark hair before he spun around, found them gathered around, watching him with aching hunger.

But I knew, even before he reached for them, that bond was broken, too.

He held out his arms to Anastasia who sobbed softly into her hands before coming to him, not from the compulsion of his blood tie, but out of what had to be her need for comfort.

"We were certain you were gone," she whispered against his shoulder, just loud enough I overheard. "And now that you're free, it's come true."

He released her, kissed her gently. "Anastasia," he said, "do not weep for me." His hands flexed around her shoulders. "I'm in a place you cannot possibly imagine. But I hope for you. Someday." He let her go. "And do not weep for yourself, my old friend. As your former leader, I relinquish control of this blood clan to your capable hands."

"I decide who leads," Pannera snapped.

Oh no, she did *not*. I glared a moment. And she backed down.

Just push me, lady. Just try it.

Syd. Sunny's mind nudged mine. *Take Sebastian and go. I'll deal with Pannera. But I think it's best if he were out of her sight quickly.*

Probably a good idea. I tugged on him, but didn't really need to. He was already turning again, ready to leave his old life behind. Eager, really.

What had I done to him?

I meant to open the veil, to get him out of there lickity split, but his long strides carried us away, his beaming smile infectious. Through the front door and into the night. The moment we stepped out into the humid dark, he turned to me and lifted me from my feet, spinning me around before setting me down again.

Okay then. Someone was a happy boy.

"Syd," he said, all intense, face next to mine as his hands first gripped my shoulders then ran slowly down my arms. "Do you know what you've done?"

I shook my head, shivering from the contact of his power with mine, his warm—how were they warm?—hands on my skin.

He leaned away, index finger rising to stroke my jawbone. "You've freed me," he said. "My blood craving is gone."

Um, what?

He laughed, a delighted sound, like a kid having the time of his life. He hugged me again and I couldn't help hug him back as my vampire sighed her own happiness.

We've done well, she sent. *I think... Sydlynn, I think this is how vampires were meant to be.*

Not again. I pulled back from him. *The maji won't like me playing Creator*, I sent, though, in the same moment, I remembered Iepa's encouragement when I freed the werewolves of the sorcerers' control.

Do you care what the maji think? My demon's growl was full of amusement.

Well. There was that.

Sebastian's hand paused in mine, raising my left to examine the rings shining there. He didn't say anything about them, but sadness flickered over his face a moment before he bowed over my fingers and kissed them.

"My very dear friend," he said. "I can never hope to repay all you have done for me. And, I hope, for my people." Sebastian took a step back, raised one hand in salute. "There will come a time and place, Sydlynn Hayle, when perhaps what I once hoped for can come to pass. Until then, be well. And be loved."

He flickered, but not into shadow like a vampire. Into a rainbow of sparking fire. And vanished.

"I take it you two were an item?" Piers's dry humor snapped me out of the little ball of sorrow I found myself in.

Holy hell, woman. You just got married twenty-four hours ago. Yes, the delicious vampire is yummynom. But you have a husband.

At home.

Waiting for you.

I turned to Piers with a smile and punched him in the chest as hard as I could.

"Mind your own business," I said, still grinning. Reached for Charlotte's hand as he rubbed his wounded pride and person with a sullen frown. "You can find your own way home?"

And left him there.

Smartass deserved it.

We appeared in the kitchen, my werefriend releasing me as we did. Hung her head.

"I'm sorry I lost Celeste."

Right. Grumble. "Not your fault," I said as Liam looked up from the large book he hunched over, sprawled out at the kitchen table.

"It is," my werefriend growled. "I don't know how she evaded me."

Funny how the sight of Liam's head cocked to one side, slight concern on his handsome face, drove worry about Celeste Oberman from my mind.

"Let Pannera's people hunt her," I said. Shrugged. She felt inconsequential to me now. Like a loose end I'd eventually wrap up when I felt like it. "She's cut herself off from all support, aside from the Brotherhood. And without a power base to offer, it's likely she's no good to them anymore. When I find the time, the two of us will go hunting."

Charlotte snarled a smile. "Can I kill her?"

"We'll talk about it." I hugged the wereprincess who bowed her head to Liam before slipping past me with, leaving my husband and I alone.

I went right to him, sank into his lap. Kissed him

firmly before snuggling into the strength of his arms and the welcome embrace of his power.

Home. Where I was meant to be.

"Great first day of marriage," I said. "How was your night, dear?"

He chuckled, the sound vibrating in my ear. "Much less exciting than yours, I imagine." He kissed the top of my head, resting his cheek on my hair. "Want to talk about it?"

Sebastian's face flashed in my mind, a surge of heat that drove a blush to my cheeks. I leaped from Liam's arms and dragged him up before jumping and wrapping my legs around his hips.

"Bed first," I said. "Then, maybe."

Liam didn't argue.

Wonder why?

Snort.

I lay in the darkness of my room, watching my husband sleep, shivering a little when my mind used the word. Amazing, I was married. And I loved him so much.

So my body had other ideas from time to time. I was pretty sure finding a hot vampire like Sebastian attractive had to be normal. But my heart was Liam's.

And that was all that mattered.

A pinch of guilt struck me, forcing me to roll over and focus. *Mom.*

Sweetheart. She answered me immediately, the image of her sitting at her desk, a single light beside her, making me sad.

You should be in bed, I sent, worried about her now. She might be whole again, and mine, but I knew she suffered still, blamed herself. Worked herself too hard to try to make up for the effects of the Brotherhood possession.

So should you, she sent.

I giggled behind my hands so as not to wake Liam. *I am.*

Mom's wicked laugh made me giggle harder.

I take it you had some success this evening? I could feel her rise, heard the click of the light as she turned it off, knew she was taking my advice.

I filled her in as she prepared for bed, shielding herself from me until I felt her, at last, sink under the sheets.

Well done, Syd, she sent. *Though I wonder what this will mean for Sebastian and all vampires. Do you think you could recreate what you've done?*

My vampire answered, quiet and thoughtful. *Unknown*, she sent to Mom. *And I'm not sure it will be necessary.*

What do you mean? Mom's mind hugged me as she spoke to my vampire ego.

That perhaps Sydlynn granted him the means to heal others of the undead, she sent. *That in granting him maji power, as she did the werewolves, she's not only created a new race, but the means to alter those meant to develop as he has now done.*

Through blood? I let my hands fall. *But he doesn't crave it anymore.*

No, my vampire sent. *Through a better, more efficient means. Through magic.*

Mom and I both fell silent as my demon and Shaylee listened, waiting.

Whatever the case, Mom sent, *Sebastian is free. And he has you to thank. We'll monitor his progress from here and offer aid if we can.*

If he allows it, my vampire sent. *I have a feeling Sebastian DeWinter is on a soul-quest of his own making and will only come back to us when he's worked out what he needs to.*

What of Pannera? Mom obviously wasn't talking to me. *Will she recover?*

My vampire hesitated. *I don't know*, she sent. *There is so much damage. Not just to her, but to her entire clan. She has little support, very little power left.* Another pause. *We shall see.*

And Ameline? I forced myself to relax, tension making my right knee jump, jiggling the bed. Liam didn't need to lose sleep over my stress. *Mom, she only needs demon power now. And she specifically told me she's after Meira.*

Mom's worry was as powerful as mine. *I don't know what to do*, she whispered in my head. *From what your maji guide told you, Ameline must complete her transformation to defeat the Brotherhood.*

Mom, I sent. *Not Meira.*

Her fierce agreement hit me like a blow.

No, she sent. *Not your sister. But you will likely have to help her find another source. If Iepa is to be believed.*

I wasn't the maji woman's biggest fan, but I was pretty sure the whole battle thing was going to come true whether I liked it—or whether Ameline had what she needed—or not. Thing was, if Ameline wasn't full maji in time, the results would be disastrous.

Not even kidding a little.

Still, the idea of finding and sacrificing a demon to that bitch—

Mom finally sighed in my head. *Get some sleep*, she sent. *Meira is safe on Demonicon for now. You know Ahbi will never allow Ameline to hurt your sister.* I felt her yawn. *We'll talk more in the morning. For now, snuggle that sweet husband of yours*—so much sadness in her voice—*and enjoy your night, sweetheart.*

She left me then, with my thoughts.

Like those were conducive to sleeping and everything.

I spun back to look at Liam, needing the distraction, tucking my hands under my cheek.

Just as he stirred in his sleep, murmuring my name. The same heat from the moment we were married burned suddenly in the base of my stomach, radiating out across my pelvis, into my thigh muscles. I welcomed it, embraced it, the subtle earth magic grounding me to Liam like nothing else ever had.

The warmth made me sleepy and, finally, my eyes drifted closed, fingers reaching out to twine loosely through Liam's.

Waking suddenly to the feeling of emptiness breaking the family wards, a mental voice calling my name in frantic need.

No rest for the wicked.

chapter ten

I leaped out of bed, Liam starting awake as I stumbled over the end of the bed and almost landed on my face. I jerked on a robe, ignoring him in my headlong flight out the door, still tying the thin terry over my naked body, and down the stairs, using magic to practically float down to the first floor.

I knew it was Piers before I turned the corner in the dark hall and entered the kitchen, just registering the fact he wasn't alone when I felt Enforcer magic reach through the emptiness of his sorcery.

And gaped at Varity Rhodes, collapsing on one of my kitchen chairs, falling from Piers's supporting grip. Both looked ashen-faced, feeling weaker than normal, my Steam Union friend's power crisping and powdering around the edges.

"What the hell?" I skidded to a halt, Liam impacting

my back when I did. I hadn't noticed he followed me downstairs I was so intent on finding out what was going on.

"Syd." Piers panted, leaning on Varity's chair as the old Enforcer Leader sagged forward, face covered in her hands. "We need your help." He caught another breath. "Els." Right. Ellis Lowsley. His partner in crime and best friend. Redheads. Always getting in trouble. "The girls." I remembered girls. Sucked at names, though the images of a blonde and a brunette flashed in my memory. "They're still at the stronghold and the Brotherhood have them. We have to go back and save them."

Um. What?

"They're where?" Shenka joined us in silence, her magic connecting with mine as she slipped into the kitchen, her own robe tucked around her. I stared back and forth between Piers and Varity, anxiety waking up, understanding rising. "Oh. My. Swearword." Anger flared, temper my favorite reaction to fear. "You two." I jabbed a finger at Piers. "You went to the stronghold plane."

Varity groaned softly, dropped her hands. Met my eyes. Hers filled with remorse. "Syd," she said. "I'm an old fool."

"Yes," I snapped as Sassafras leaped up onto the table, tail thrashing. "You are. A total and utter idiot." I spun on Piers, fire crackling as my demon snarled her irritation, fear still fighting to win through anger. "And you." I wanted to shake him, smack him. "What the hell, Piers?"

Hard to be articulate when I could barely think past my need to kick his freaking ass.

He tried to scowl. Lost it in regret. "I know," he said, turning to pace away from the table, hands wringing. "It was stupid. But I had to do something." He turned back to me, long, blonde hair swinging in a silk wave. "We had to do something." His hands dropped, shoulders slouching. "It was just meant to be a recon mission."

Sassafras hissed, amber fire lighting his eyes as I bit back the string of curses I usually only used in my head and drew a breath.

"Tell me someone with authority knew you two were up to no good." His mother. Mine. Enforcer Leader Pender Tremere. Someone.

Anyone.

Piers's misery, Varity's silence. Both answered me loud and clear.

"Arrogant children," Sassafras snarled.

I groaned and sank into a chair, anger rushing out of me as I tried to absorb this latest disaster.

"Tell me everything," I said.

"We don't have time." Agony crossed his handsome face, lit his gray eyes. "The Brotherhood has my friends, Syd."

"I'm not running off to save them unless I know exactly what you were up to," I said. Because half-cocked wasn't my normal way of business.

Yeah, right.

Piers glared a moment before jerking out a chair and dropping himself into it as the scent of fresh coffee filled the kitchen. Bless Shenka, she started delivering hot, black cups all around as Piers began his sordid little tale.

"We wanted you in on this from the beginning," Piers said, leaning toward me over his steaming cup. "And I had every intention of telling you, I really did."

Varity sighed, shook her head. "I'm sorry, Syd," she said. "I don't know what I was thinking."

Piers reached over and squeezed her hand. "I talked you into it," he said. "The fault is all mine."

I knew how persuasive he could be and gave Varity the benefit of the doubt as I crossed my legs and my arms over my chest, one foot bobbing in agitation while my fingers tapped on my bicep. Because just one action wasn't enough to release the building frustration I felt.

Not nearly enough.

"We never intended to take on the Brotherhood," Piers said, all earnest. Uh-huh. "I thought if we could sneak inside, have a look around, check out their numbers, their positioning inside the stronghold, we could get a better idea of what we were up against when the Enforcers decided to attack."

Freaking idiot. "Failing to realize," I said with a snarl, "we already have a spy inside the Brotherhood." Well, not technically true at the moment, but I had no doubt if Demetrius wanted to return to the stronghold plane, he could. And do a damned better job of it than this young moron.

Piers flinched. "We're sane," he said.

"Debatable," I snapped back. Forced myself to calm. The Enforcers wouldn't stand a chance against the Brotherhood at this point. "With the stronghold under Brotherhood control," I said, "the Enforcers would be seen as the enemy to the protections guarding it." I looked to Varity for confirmation. She shrugged. "Okay, so we don't know that. But regardless, they wouldn't stand a chance against sorcerers and you know it. What makes you think they're going to try an all-out assault when such an attack is already off the playlist?"

Mom's orders.

I ground my teeth, hearing the squeak telling me I'd lost another layer of enamel. "Why you ever thought I'd agree to go—"

He shrugged, Varity staring into her coffee.

"He came to me just after conclave," Varity said. "We've all been so upset, Syd. Worked up about the loss. It's personal for us, for the Enforcer order." She shook her head. "I almost didn't listen to young Piers here."

There was that stupid honor thing again. The next

person who brought it up to me was going to get a firm whack upside the head.

"You had your orders, Enforcer," I said, keeping my tone cold. "Your Council Leader told all of you to stand down. To leave this to me."

Varity's eyes narrowed. "Technically not true," she said. "I'm not on active rolls anymore. So the order didn't really apply to me."

Sigh. Double sigh. Freaking triple, quadruple, endless sigh.

"Varity," I said, all the weight of my disapproval in my voice.

She cracked a grin, weak and sorrowful, but a grin. "Yeah," she said. "I know."

"Mum refused to talk about it." Piers's frustration came through in his words. Knowing Eva Southway, I wasn't surprised. "And we knew we couldn't ask Pender. He might be tearing himself up inside over the loss of the stronghold, but he's too much a stickler for law to go against your mother."

And Mom was out, without saying.

Piers went on. "I needed an Enforcer," he said. "And Varity seemed the perfect choice."

"The back doors into the stronghold." The Brotherhood hadn't been able to access them, only the main mirror entry. That was why they needed to liberate one of the shards to trigger it.

Varity nodded. "Worked for me when we fought the Brotherhood during conclave," she said.

She was right. She'd snuck in, helped me break the sorcerous hold over Margaret Applegate by severing Vasyl Krajnik's connection to the stronghold and its vast power. Just before the wild magicks killed him.

"You had to know they must have hunted those back doors down by now." Were these two really that stupid? Because, if I were Belaisle—shuddershivergrossness—I would have done so the moment I lost my little pawn on this plane with the death of Vasyl.

Piers's shoulders sagged. "We checked them out," he said. "They were all intact."

Just like Belaisle. "Traps," I said.

Varity nodded, heavy with guilt. "I led them right into an ambush, Syd," she said. "Little lambs to the slaughter."

My stomach clenched, heart speeding up. "They're dead?" But Piers said—

"Just a figure of speech," Varity said. "Sorry."

Sassafras's tail hit my ribs as he lashed it back and forth. "Varity Rhodes," he said. "I have never been more ashamed of you. You know better."

She didn't say anything, returning her gaze to her now cooling coffee.

Sass turned to me, flames snapping around him. "We must alert your mother. At once." He glanced sideways at Piers. "And Eva Southway. Both must be prepared for possible repercussions."

"Not to mention the chance the Brotherhood could gain valuable information from your friends." Piers's miserable nod affirmed that little fact. "Piers, I understand your need to help, but this? Why this attempt at playing hero?"

His jaw clenched. "Because they've taken enough from us, Syd," he said. "And I'm done letting them think it's okay."

I let my arms drop, hands gripping the edge of the table in an effort not to fling them in the air and wash myself of this problem. "You two are in so much trouble, you have no idea."

Piers pushed his chair back, legs bobbing, tense and eager. "We really need to go," he said. "While Els and the girls were alive when we managed to escape, I can't be sure they'll stay that way." Tears rose in his eyes. "I should never have left them," he whispered. Turned to Varity. "Why did I leave them?"

She patted his shoulder with one thin hand, sorrow on her face. "We didn't have a choice," she said. "If we'd stayed, no one would know they are prisoners. I should have remained to fight, though, you're right about that. Only one of us needed to come back."

He shook his head with fierce intensity. "I had to have your power you to cross back to Harvard," he said. Drew a breath and sank back into his chair. "We both had to go."

Varity's little smile made me wonder just how fantastic a leader she'd been. A phenom, I was sure of it. Too bad she fell in with disruptive company.

Considering how much trouble I myself created over the years, I finally let go of my anger and cut them some slack. Wasn't doing me any good anyway. And I had people to alert.

"One last question," Sassafras said. "Why didn't you approach Syd?"

I forgot about that. Paused before reaching for Mom.

Piers's wry grin was a good match for the defeat on his face. "I tried," he said. "Several times. Including tagging along with you tonight." His fingers wound together in his lap as he lowered his gaze to watch what he was doing. "When you left me at the mansion, I figured I was out of options." He looked up again. "We were on a deadline, wanted to go in tonight."

"Nice last minute recruiting," I said.

"Figured if I gave you no time to think about it, you'd fall into place." He shook his head, met Liam's eyes. "You're in for a hell of a marriage, my friend."

My husband smiled, arm slipping around my shoulders. "Every day is an adventure," he said.

Hardy har har.

I turned away from the others, rising to leave the kitchen, retreating to the quiet, dark hall as the front door opened and the feeling of Trill's power entered. I left Piers to explain himself to my maji friend and reached for Mom.

Was really, really looking forward to waking her up with this.

chapter eleven

Mom's reaction was as expected.

What the bloody hell were they thinking? I could feel her jerking back her covers, stomping out of bed and to her office, mind splitting as she reached for the Council. *Syd, this is a disaster. If the Brotherhood has access to sensitive Steam Union information, they could be at great risk for attack, even now. How much do those kids know?*

From what Piers implied, enough.

Mom cursed.

I know. My anger had mostly burned out, hers making me tired. *But we can't just leave them there.*

Why not, if their foolishness has already given up their people? Her growl of fury turned to a sigh. *Damn that boy,* she sent. *I'm so glad you didn't marry him, Syd. I just couldn't take two of you in my family.*

Snort. *Thanks, Mom,* I sent.

She laughed, breathless, sinking into her chair behind her desk. *I'll alert Eva Southway*, she sent.

Appreciate it, I sent. *As much as I didn't want to tell you, I really wasn't looking forward to that particular conversation.*

Thanks. Mom's dry tone made me chuckle. *Oh, Syd*, she sent. *Do you think we'll ever come to a time when the world doesn't feel like it's about to end?*

I hope not, I sent. *Then what would we do?*

I've always wanted to learn to knit, she sent.

We laughed together, the amusement of two people pushed to the edge too often and used to jumping in anyway.

I love you, she sent. *Please be careful. And bring those kids back.*

Um. Wow. *I have permission to rescue them?*

Mom hugged me before letting me go. *You do*, she sent. *And the Brotherhood be damned. But Syd, please remember, our plane is in one piece. I'd like to keep it that way for as long as possible.*

Hell yeah.

I let Mom go, tingling with excitement all of a sudden. No, I didn't have Ameline. And shouldn't be contemplating what I was contemplating. The very idea of going to the stronghold was stupid, irresponsible, went against my fate. And yet.

And yet.

The opportunity to kick some Brotherhood ass was

just so tempting.

You're as bad as that Southway boy, Sassafras sent.

Eavesdropper. I turned and found him standing behind me, the sound of talking coming from the kitchen, the light illuminating him in a back glow in the dark hall. Only the pinpoints of amber fire that were his eyes showed clearly as he watched me.

You're not seriously considering this. He growled softly, body shaking from it. *Syd.*

Sass. I bent and scooped him into my arms, trying to cuddle him while he hissed and struggled. *Who else is there?*

He finally fell still. *You would have gone with them, wouldn't you? If he'd found a way to ask?*

Aw, hell. *I don't know*, I sent. *Maybe.*

Liar.

You are our hope against the Brotherhood, Sass sent, paws pressing to my cheeks. *And I don't think cheating is going to be allowed. You be careful.*

I will. I kissed his forehead, the soft fur tickling my nose. *I promise.*

As I carried him into the kitchen, I felt my burst of enthusiasm fade to nerves. Sass was right, of course. My arguments to myself about how I could handle this myself, without Ameline, maybe change my destiny fell short, rang hollow.

Damn it.

I looked up to find Trill staring at me, Owen and

Apollo behind her. All looked rather determined. Which made me suddenly nervous.

"Absolutely not," I said, setting Sassafras on the table. "You three are staying put."

"Make us." Trill stomped one foot, arms crossed over her chest as Owen mimicked her. Even Apollo, typically smirking and joking, looked like he'd been transformed into a stone statue. A very stern stone statue.

"Trill." Was I surrounded by adventure seeking, honor loving bratskis?

"Syd." Trill set one hand on Varity's shoulder. "When do we leave?"

"Fine." I wasn't going to win, knew it, felt her stubbornness. Knew her well enough I could already see her following me regardless of what I wanted. "But we need more than you three if this is going to work."

I hated the thought of involving him. Didn't want to see him again, not so soon. But there was no way I was taking Varity with me and I needed an Enforcer, didn't I?

Liam looked up at me, a little frown on his face as my mind reached for his.

I'm sorry, I sent. *But I have to call Quaid.*

His frown smoothed out instantly, hand reaching for mine.

He's the best choice, Liam sent. *And I want you to be safe. So Quaid it is.*

I loved my husband.

Quaid. I felt his power snap into place with mine the moment I reached for him.

Syd. Was that a hint of panic? Sure was. *What's wrong?* Probably because he knew I'd only be calling if there was an emergency.

This qualified.

I need your help, I sent without a hint of ego. No time for our little back and forth battle. Besides, I was married now. The part of my life involving Quaid and my heart was over. Time to create a professional relationship in its place.

Sure, Syd. Keep telling yourself it's just work.

Sigh.

I'm on my way. He cut me off, power flaring just before he did. I barely had time to turn to Varity when Quaid's magic broke through the family wards and he stepped through the kitchen door.

She took one look at him and snapped a scowl at me. "You're not leaving me behind," she said.

"I am." I pushed her down with power when she tried to rise. "You are going to Mom and explain every single thing that happened." Her rebellion pushed against me, but I was far stronger. "Varity," I said, softer, with kindness. "Please. I really need you to do this for me."

She hesitated, shoulders slumping. "I suppose a stronger, younger Enforcer might be a better choice," she said, voice crisp.

I crossed the kitchen, at her side in three steps, gripping her arms in my hands. Shook her just enough she straightened. "I need you," I said. "And so does Mom."

A little smile broke at the edge of her mouth. "You don't have to try to make a foolish old lady feel better, girl."

"I'm not," I said, stepping back. "I'm asking a former Enforcer Leader to inform her Council Leader of all the details and keep her up-to-date on what we're doing." I looked at Quaid. "Because I'm assuming you can link up with Enforcer Tinder here in real time?"

Varity turned to Quaid, nodding thoughtfully. "Brilliant," she said. Smiled for real this time before saluting. "Be safe," she said, blue fire flaring around her, vanishing into it as the family magic allowed her the courtesy to leave with her pride.

"Now," I said, turning toward the hall again, "if someone could fill in Quaid, I have to go put on some clothes."

Because invading the stronghold in my robe wasn't on my list of to-dos at the moment, thanks.

Liam joined me, sitting on the edge of the bed as I jerked on a pair of jeans, cursing over the clasps of my bra. He laughed, came to help, strong fingers connecting the hooks for me, smoothing the straps over my shoulders. His lips brushed across my neck, hands lifting my hair free, making me shiver all the way down my spine.

I turned and hugged him, face pressed to his bare chest, breathing in his scent, making it part of me. "I love you."

He nodded against the top of my head. "I love you, too." Liam leaned away, grabbed a t-shirt, held it out to me. "Don't you have a world to save or something?"

I laughed, pulling the soft fabric over my head, scooping my hair out from under the collar before nabbing an elastic for the heavy stuff. "Just a few idiot sorcerers," I said. "Slow day."

Liam's chuckle held my grin in place until he kissed me. "I'll be here," he said without a trace of resentment or envy.

And didn't tell me to be careful.

The. Best. Husband. Ever.

Back in the kitchen, I outlined my hastily prepared plan. As in, I came up with it while walking down the stairs still twisting my hair into a knot at the back of my head.

"We stay together," I said. "No heroics, no running off to get revenge for anything." That was for me, mostly. And Quaid. Though who knew what Belaisle did to Trill and her brothers? From the tightening of Apollo's face, he must have thought I was talking to him. "I cut the veil," okay, would try to, but was pretty sure it would work, "so we show up where the Brotherhood won't expect. Quaid," I turned to him, "you know the stronghold," I'd only been there a couple of times, mostly just to prison. "I'll need you to navigate us and keep us from running into trouble if Piers can't do his part."

He nodded brusquely, no comment.

Good solider.

"Piers," I focused on the now trembling Steam Union sorcerer, his eagerness to move clouding him, I was sure of it. "Pay attention." Sassafras snorted behind me and I almost laughed. Wasn't that his favorite thing to say to me? And Gram's? Piers shivered, but jerked a nod. "As soon as we arrive, I want you to tell Quaid exactly where your friends are and find them. Once we know and he can show me, we veil in, grab them," hopefully with very little fight, "and veil out again." I was, of course, running on the supposition the Steam Union members weren't being held in a place shielded from my power. And that Piers could find them amid all the sorcery.

While I was sure I could figure out how to ride the emptiness as Demetrius did if I didn't have access to Ahbi, I didn't really want to repeat the experience.

That left my determined trio.

"Trill and company," I scowled at the Zornovs, "aren't necessary, so you stay behind me and be good or I'll kill the three of you myself."

"I beg to differ," Apollo said. "We can track the

movements of the Brotherhood while Piers focuses on his friends."

Trill looked smug. "So there," she said, though I was certain she had no idea Apollo had such a plan in mind until he spoke up just then.

Owen just grinned and winked at me.

Bratskis. To the bone.

"Okay, you lot." I turned and hugged Shenka, kissed Liam one last time, ruffled Sassafras's fur. Finally spun on my motley crew. "Shall we?"

Because, there really was no time like the present for a little mayhem.

I reached for the veil, felt Ahbi's touch. Showed her where I needed to go. And, with a flare of amber magic, stepped into the veil.

chapter twelve

Ahbi released us at the base of the prison tower, the bottom of the steps a familiar sight I'd climbed twice and, hopefully, would never have to again.

My thighs trembled at the memory of all those stairs.

Quaid grinned at me for my choice.

"Perfect," he said, speaking in a whisper and, for the first time, I remembered using mental connections and any magic, really, would trigger the stronghold's protective magic. Not to hurt us or anything, at least not here, from what Gram told me. But would trigger warnings of the Brotherhood we were around. The veil was different, the power contained inside it, so riding it wasn't an issue. But any overt, outward magic could create some serious problems.

Good thing one of us was thinking.

"I thought so," I whispered back. "Didn't think

there'd be much activity here." At least, hoped. Who knew if the Brotherhood thought some back way into the prison tower was important just because the Enforcers hadn't?

Piers's face screwed up in a desperate scowl before he shook his head. "I can feel them," he said. "But I can't see where they are."

Trill reached for his hand. "Let me."

Risky. I almost warned her against it. But she wasn't alone, Owen connecting with her, then Apollo gripping his brother's fingers tightly. Owen's eyes turned black as the Zornovs eased their way into Piers's mind.

Trill closed hers a moment before turning and opening them again, eyes glowing with iridescence as she focused on Quaid.

"Here," she whispered.

He touched her cheek, a spark passing between them. Quaid frowned, nodded. Looked at me.

And his expression wasn't what I was hoping for.

"I know where they are," he said. "You're not going to like it."

And looked up the stairs.

Damn it.

"You're kidding me, right?" I rubbed my thighs and winced in anticipation. No way could I ride the veil up there without alerting every single Brotherhood member we were around. If they didn't know already. The amount of protection magic built into the top of the tower didn't allow any energy to go undetected.

I really hated Piers right about now.

We trudged up the steps, Quaid taking the rear while I led, drawing on the innate strength of my alter egos to keep me from collapsing. I'd given up running in the last year or so, gotten a bit flabby, if truth be told. No more. As soon as I got home, I was starting again.

And never stopping. Because, honestly, since there were more than enough times my power wasn't available to save me in the past, running was a skill I really needed to keep up in my line of work.

Trill hissed at me about three quarters of the way to the top. She eased past the others, the rail-less steps just wide enough for her to make it to my side.

"Someone's coming," she whispered. The echoing sound of approaching feet reinforced her warning. Quaid made his way to us at the same moment, leaning past her.

"I've been waiting for this," he said. "I'm going to try a trick. Just hold still."

Um, what?

Before I could argue, he had turned, whispered down the line. Everyone froze, backs to the wall as Quaid pressed one palm to the stone and closed his eyes.

Melting from sight as though the very stronghold absorbed him.

Trill was next, Owen, with huge eyes. Apollo. Piers. I

looked down at myself, felt cool rock even through my temperature numbness, felt my body solidify, quiet, still.

As stone.

Just in time. A dozen black-robed sorcerers entered the base of the tower, looking up the stairs. I could see them still, as though through a haze of dust. They talked among themselves, too far away and muffled from the rock's embrace for me to make them out clearly. Felt the brush of emptiness over me, but I was stone, nothing to see here, move along.

We must have triggered some kind of alert, maybe mild, but enough Belaisle thought to send some of his goons to check. They talked another moment before leaving, their footsteps echoing until they passed through the arched stone doorway and were gone.

Quaid waited what felt like forever before releasing us. I started counting part way through the pause, my mind's compulsive need to know how much time passed reaching fifty before my body limbered and I stepped away from the wall with a deep breath of air.

Turned to Quaid and gently bumped his shoulder. "Nice job."

His smirk was as familiar as the chocolate of his eyes. "Varity actually taught me that one," he said. He patted the wall with some affection. "No magic involved, at least, not mine. The power of the stronghold likes us for some reason, wants us to be part of it. She said she stumbled on it when she was a trainee, trying to hide from one of her instructors." I snorted, unsurprised. "Nice to know the old boy still recognizes Enforcers."

It had to be hard for him. But if I had anything to say about it, the Enforcers would have their plane back again. And soon.

But not today. Today was about rescuing some idiots. Right.

The last bit of climb was easier, thanks to the brief rest playing rock. I wasn't a panting mess at the top, at least. Stepped aside for Quaid who eased the door open and peeked inside.

"Any way you can use that rock trick to get us around?" Would be slick.

He shook his head. "Have to be stationary," he said. "Shhh."

Did he just shush me?

Grrr.

Oh. Someone was coming. Okay then.

The door closed softly under Quaid's hand, only the barest crack remaining. I peeked through it, my head tucked under his chin, watched as a pair of Brotherhood sorcerers passed.

"Here's the thing," I said, turning to the others with my voice hopefully only loud enough for us to hear. "I have no idea what the stronghold will do to me if I try to open the veil in there." My thumb jerked over my shoulder toward the circle of cells just beyond the door. Quaid shrugged, shook his head. No help there. "So, the plan is, get to Piers's friends. Fighting is physical only, no magic." So sucked. And yet, I assumed the sorcerers might be in the same boat. The protections around the stronghold were pretty formidable. Still, it might just serve to feed the Brotherhood during an attack. I had no way of knowing.

This was so risky it just screamed a Sydlynn Hayle caper.

"Once we have them, I'm going to try to open the veil." Knowing there were a million go-wrong variables, from the stronghold attacking and destabilizing the Node through Ahbi to being attacked myself, to the Brotherhood becoming super-powerful because I unleashed the power of the stronghold all swirled in my head, argument piled on argument while I went on. "And we haul ass." I pinned Piers with a glare. "One shot, this is it. We fail and it's all over, sunshine. Your friends are on their own."

He grunted as though I'd slapped him, but nodded.

Like I'd ever leave anyone behind.

Damned honor and crap.

"Here we go. Stay together, and remember, no magic."

Trill moved up beside me, hand holding Owen's. "We'll let you know when it's safe," she whispered.

Paused. Shook her head, again. Then nodded with a soft whistle of released air. "Now. Go."

And we were going. Into the curved stone hall, Quaid beside me, Trill close behind, Piers passing cells, looking inside even though I knew they were empty.

Knew exactly where the Steam Union sorcerers were being held. The only logical place.

My old cell loomed before us around the corner, a pair of Brotherhood sorcerers talking in front of it. Didn't see us, fortunately, Quaid holding Trill back as she popped around the curve.

Piers peeked, turned to me and made an okay sign with his finger and thumb in a circle. I'd guessed right. Good for me.

Trill's eyes flew wide as she spun and poked me at the same time.

No translation necessary.

We were about to have company.

chapter Thirteen

I may not have been running, but I still beat up the heavy bag on an almost daily basis, my fighting skills much improved thanks to my martial arts training with my normal instructor, Sage. I think he would have been proud of me as I leaped out of hiding and headed for my target, Brotherhood Goon #1, taking the tall, heavy-shouldered man full in the chest with both feet. He crashed backward into the door, head hitting stone with the hollow sound of a rotten gourd being smashed and collapsed where he stood, whites of his eyes showing.

Boo-ya.

Quaid made short work of his little playmate, Brotherhood Goon #2 hitting the ground about a second after my target lost his touch with reality. But I could hear shouting from behind me and knew time was short.

When wasn't it?

The cell door crashed open with an echoing bang, the metal and wood impacting rock so loudly the four Brotherhood sorcerers inside actually jumped from the sound. I was already moving, attacking one with an uppercut, making my knuckles burn before sweeping his feet out from under him with a kick to the side of his knee.

I spun, caught sight of Piers bending over one of three narrow cots in the room where once there had only been one, red hair and freckles of the unconscious victim he crouched beside identifying him as Ellis Lowsley, Piers's best friend and co-conspirator in all things mind your own business. Two girls, both faces I recognized, even if I couldn't take the time required to hunt up names, lay on the other cots, also out cold.

Quaid's next opponent was already down, but he was busy with the Zornovs at the door, trying to keep what looked like a sea of black robes from crashing into the room. The other two sorcerers went down quickly and, as I hoped, neither tried to use sorcery on me.

The stronghold's protections prevented them, too. Which made me wonder if the stronghold really was theirs after all. Wouldn't it welcome them if that were the case?

Things that made me go hmmm would have to wait until my friends were safe.

Not working out very well at the moment.

"Quaid!" I called to him as I turned, the last of my enemies dropping to his knees, then his side, a huge lump rising on his temple from a blow of my fist. Belaisle hadn't trained his interrogators in hand-to-hand, clearly. Good for me. I just wished it was the same for his hulking bullies. Quaid was gone out the door, surrounded by Brotherhood, the Zornovs nowhere to be seen. I sprinted for the exit, only to have Piers beat me to it, slamming it in the face of a sorcerer who tried to enter.

The sound of his face thudding into the other side did nothing to chill my rage as I reached for the door to jerk it open again.

Piers held me off, face twisted in anxiety. "Send them home first," he said. "Then we'll go after the others."

Was he freaking kidding me? Rage flared, poured over me like a boiling pot of oil so hot I was sure I'd burst into flames at any second.

"So your friends are more important than mine," I said. Lashed out and punched him in the chest. Same spot as last time, only harder, much harder. So hard, he gasped for air.

"Syd," he choked. "Please. I'll stay and help you, but they are hurt. They have to go home."

Damn him. Damn him!

I spun, reached for the veil. Felt the stronghold respond, power rushing toward me, not enough time to catch Ahbi, to open the veil and escape.

Unless. Quaid called it a "him", hadn't he? Old boy, he said. Liked Enforcers, he said.

And acted on impulse.

Please, I sent to the power rushing to crush me for my invasion. *Please, help me.*

Pause. Recognition. Retreat.

It actually worked?

Ahbi found me, opened the veil while I sobbed once in relief, not knowing why or how the stronghold gave me leeway, but not willing to waste it. Please. I'd have to use it more often.

I grabbed the three fallen sorcerers, tossed them into the veil, before latching onto Piers with my power and heaving him toward the opening.

Ahbi, I sent, *can you take them without me?*

Yes, she sent. And they were gone, Piers screaming my name as the veil sealed around him.

I spun, dashed for the door. Used my power to slam it open.

Met resistance so powerful I was sure Belaisle caught me, trapped me here.

Until the curious mind of the stronghold touched mine and I froze.

Maji, he sent. Definite "he" to the flavor of the place, all grinding stone and depth of power. Quaid was right. *Light One. Welcome back.*

Holy. Freaking. Crap.

Hi? Syd. Come on. You can do so much better than that while your friend's lives are at stake.

The stronghold's power ground together, the sound of rock crushing in my head. *I've been waiting for your return,* he sent. *Have missed you. Not the Dark One.* His anger felt as deep as the heart of the plane and as old as the Universe, slow to rise but scaring the crap out of me none the less. *She, I can do without.*

Makes two of us, I sent. Giggled in mild hysteria and jerked myself back to focus. *Thank you for letting me open the veil,* I sent.

Yes, he sent. *You had need. And though this is the center of my power and doing so put me at risk, I knew you meant only good, not ill.*

This tower? I didn't even try to hide my surprise. *Why here?*

My heart lies beneath us, he sent. *Under the stone. At the base of this spike.*

Cool. Very cool. And yet, I really didn't have time to do show and tell at the moment. *I have to save my friends,* I sent. *The Brotherhood has them.* Terror roared to life in my stomach. I had no doubt Belaisle would know about it by now, they could even be in his custody already.

Trill. Owen. Apollo. He'd hunted them before, wanted them to fulfill a prophecy. Damn it, had I just delivered them to him? To it?

And Quaid.

Would not. Could not.

So much fear.

The empty ones, the stronghold grated in anger, *they are not welcome here.*

Can you kick them out? Hope, could it be?

I cannot, he sent, stone groaning in protest. *I remember them, their greed, feeding from me when I have another destiny.* I could hear pounding at the door, but felt nothing, not a trace of sorcery reaching through the stronghold's protections. *I can only wait for the time to come when what must be either is or isn't.*

Cryptic. Just lovely. I hated cryptic.

And yet, I found myself calming, slowing down, connecting with the stronghold.

Can you help me? Already was, keeping me safe up here. And if I could continue to ride the veil in the stronghold itself without being squashed like a bug, that would rock.

No pun intended.

I cannot act on your behalf, he sent with the regret of an immobile mountain, *but I can ensure you are allowed to act without bias.*

Me and my new bestie thought alike, sure did.

Too bad he was a big, stone castle.

I'd take him.

Thank you, I sent, spinning to the door, maji power rising in full-blown fury. Hit the door with a blast of creation power dissolving the exit, the wall beside it and probably sent several of the Brotherhood behind it into low orbit.

Impressive, the stronghold sent.

I caught myself grinning. Damn it, Syd. Not funny.

Or fun. Sure. Not fun at all.

Ahbi's presence put an end to my smirk just as I passed over the threshold and into the blackened mess of the prison hall. Demon magic surged through the tear a heartbeat before Meira's mind reached mine.

SYD!

Meems! Ameline. Oh. My. Swear—

No. Not now. Not when everything hung in the balance for my friends. But how could I say no? I couldn't. Simple as that.

Please, I sent to the stronghold as I spun and ran for the veil opening. *I know you can't save them, but do what you can to protect my friends.*

So thin, weak, empty, my attempt to help them while choosing my sister over their safety. Because I really had no choice.

His affirmation made me feel a little better. Only a little. Terror and guilt and absolute loathing filled me as I promised to come back for them, knowing now I could, before throwing myself through the gap after my desperate sister.

Mind locked on Meira, hyper-focus channeled into saving her from whoever dared attack her.

chapter fourteen

Ahbi's power engulfed me, her panic as powerful as mine, mixed with so much rage I felt my skin crackle under the fire of her fury even as she dumped me out the other side with a flare of warning.

I flew out of the gap on the Demonicon side, body bursting into full demon form, my maji power crackling. I was already pissed off, scared and full of hate. If Ameline found a way to come at my sister anyway, I didn't care if all the planes fell.

I'd kill her with my bare hands.

And then go back and save Quaid and the Zornovs.

I had one second to see my sister fighting off a pack of attackers, a roar of absolute rage shaking my entire body as my demon's fire blazed around me, shoving down my other egos in her need to reach Meira.

The next second, I felt the dull numbness of impact

against the back of my skull and fell, screaming my fury, into darkness.

Pain registered first, flaring like a volcano before ebbing backward as my spirit power healed me. Groggy, twinging with the remains of my anger, I struggled to remember what happened.

Ahbi's power crashed into me as my grandmother's spirit woke me the rest of the way with a not-so-subtle kick in the ass. I felt myself spinning sideways, lost in the veil. Had I somehow opened the way again after I was hit? But where was Meira? No way would I abandon my sister.

No. Way.

Hang on. I'd abandoned someone… hadn't I? Not Meira, never her.

Who then did I leave behind?

The veil parted without warning, dumping me out onto hard stone, tumbling out onto my shoulder feeling totally disoriented. I landed with a thud, breath catching as pain surged across my back, easing again a moment later.

Wind rushed over me, chill, though the temperature only just registered, the cold stone beneath me black and sharp and shining. I rolled over with a groan, looked up.

Almost died right then and there.

The edge of the peak cut off beneath my chin, long,

long drop stretching out beneath me—

—*I fell and fell, heart ready to explode, lungs unable to catch air, the Parade growing larger as I plummeted to my death*—

I gasped and pulled back, wobbly from the blow to my head, from vertigo as I scrambled in reverse on my hands and feet, picking up speed as I panted for breath.

Ran into something hard.

Looked up.

A dark shape loomed over me, bending just a little, shining, sparkling eyes shimmering in the light of the moons above.

Holy. Freaking. Hell.

Was this one of the attackers who went after my sister? Panic and fear fought a losing battle with my anger as I wrapped myself in maji power and pushed up onto my very human feet, demon form gone in place of my natural state.

He still loomed over me, though, now his face was no longer in shadow, I could see he was a man. Not really, not mortal. But not demon, either. And Meira's attackers were demons, their red-tinted skin a dead giveaway.

This—whoever and whatever he was—exuded so much power I felt almost insignificant next to him. His physical presence didn't help much, shoulders twice as wide as mine, skin a soft shade of gray, bald head covered in some kind of tiny scales.

But it was his diamond eyes that captured me the

most.

Until I caught movement behind him. Glanced around.

Realized we weren't alone. But there weren't other people with us, oh no. That would have been too easy, wouldn't it?

Just my luck, the bowl-like peak I shivered on, the back end open to the darkness, was covered in dragons.

"Welcome," he said in a voice that made my entire body tremble from the depth and pitch of it. "Friend."

Several cogs wound up, clicked together, formed connections as two of the giant dragons shifted, morphed, shrank into human shape and I understood.

Remembered.

Flying in a transport with Ram, heading for Bilhaeder in my pursuit of Ameline, finding ourselves in the midst of a flight of dragons.

The lead one reaching for my mind. And calling me friend.

I shuddered, hugging myself, the pressure of his power so vast I found myself flinching from him, pushing back with my maji magic. He bowed his head, his energy retreating enough I didn't feel the urge to fall at his feet and beg him not to kill me.

Yowza.

"What are you?" I watched, heart about ready to leap out of my chest and pitch itself over the edge alone as more of the dragons shrank into human form and came to gather, to stare with their diamond eyes and press against me with the weight of their power.

"We are the drach," he said. "And we've been waiting for you."

Um. Okay.

For good reasons, I hoped. Time to pull it together, seriously. After all, Ahbi dumped me here, didn't she? And wouldn't have done so without a very good reason.

Meems. "My sister." The words came out in a gasp of need.

He nodded. "We know why you are here," he said. "But your fear the Dark One has taken the Princess is unfounded."

The Dark One? He had to mean Ameline. And yes, that was exactly where my terror went. She'd already told me she was gunning for Meira's power in an effort to complete her maji abilities. This attack, coming so soon after Ameline claimed the taint from Pannera, led me to only one obvious conclusion. Not so obvious, it seemed.

"The threat to Hathenemeira is much more mundane." I began to grow accustomed to the vibration of his voice, the overwhelming wash of his magic, able to focus at least on what he was saying.

"Who?" Coherent, mostly.

"Ruler has chosen unwisely," the dragon in human form said as the gathering behind him, some still giant and winged, others looking like him, hummed a soft song of agitation. At least, I thought it was agitation. For all I knew, they were getting ready to sing me the song of their people or something.

Hang on. Dad?

"Your sister has made herself an obstacle to one of your father's choices for mate," the hulking man-creature said. "It is this demon's attempt to remove Hathenemeira from her path which has led you here and your sister close to death."

The whole "close to death" part definitely got my attention. And triggered my temper, shoving down the last of my awe, though I remained shivery every time I remembered where I stood.

And that a long drop waited not so far away.

"Why am I here?" I took a step back from him, and to the side, keeping the edge in my peripheral vision. One of the dragons perched above me flared its wings.

"It was time we met," Mr. Chatty Pants said. "The coming of the battle has finally freed us to act. On your behalf."

A woman—okay, dragon woman—stepped forward. "And on the behalf of the Dark One." Her voice came across as a slightly more feminine version of his.

I scowled at the caveat she added.

Sounded like a pain in my ass. This whole balance thing could bite me.

He ignored her, as though she hadn't spoken. "Our tasks have come to a meeting of ways," he said. Wow. More cryptic. I was actually glad, how it fed my anger and kept me from going all gaga again.

"How nice for our tasks," I said. Snarky, hell yeah. "But I frankly don't give two shakes about fate and destiny and the Dark One crap." My demon grumbled her agreement. "In fact, at this second, all I really want to do is find my sister."

He bowed to me, as though his power couldn't have crushed mine in a snap, his people's humming shaking the ground under my feet.

"Of course," he said. Held out his hand, palm the size of a side plate. "Allow me to take you to her, Light One."

Blerg. "Syd," I said.

One of his eyebrows cocked, a shimmer of light passing over his diamond eyes. "Delightful," he said, voice no longer making my bones ache. "I am—"

Hmmm. Yeah. No way in hell I could pronounce whatever he just said.

"I'm calling you Max." I took his hand.

Had the absolute shock of my life as our power finally connected and I understood we weren't so different after all.

"You're maji," I said.

"No." Max's lips turned up into a small smile. "The maji claim the right, but the drach were first."

chapter fifteen

"Hang on," I said, hand still engulfed in his. "The Creator made the maji who formed the planes."

A rumbling song rang from the gathered dragons.

"They would have you believe so," Max said. "It was Creator's desire they be responsible for the formation of life. But we, Creator made and set free."

Random. My brain sizzled with further connections. "The wild magicks," I said, thinking of the tumbling, happy threads I'd freed from the Brotherhood, the same power that warned me about the sorcerers' takeover of the stronghold.

Max nodded as the song softened, my skin no longer crawling from the push of their power. "Our souls," he said. "What remains of us when we are done in physical form."

Oh. My. Swearword. "Those ribbons?" The flittering

butterfly-like magic I'd carried with me as they grieved. "Drach souls?"

Max's laugh was nothing like his spoken voice, reaching inside me, in harmony with my very spirit, making me smile, too.

"Their freedom was our trigger," he said. "We've been watching you since your creation, Light One—Syd." Nice I didn't have to remind him. "We knew you would come to this place, when the time was right. Fate foretold it and we have long awaited your coming."

Fate again. Sigh.

Then again, hadn't Demetrius said random needed to be free? And that random always won?

My gaze drifted to the female drach waiting behind Max with the silent patience of a statue.

Not so random, then, if Ameline and I both had access.

"The maji won't help me," I said, doing my best to keep the bitterness from my voice.

"We don't have their excuses or restraint," Max said. "We are here to serve in any way you need." His smile returned. "You remember me," he said. "I'd already told you I was a friend. But our only restriction was being forced to wait for you to come to us of your own free will."

Which hadn't exactly happened, had it? Ahbi cheated. Why wasn't I surprised? Not that I was complaining. The idea of having a dragon army to command when I crossed to the empty plane to fight Liander Belaisle made me feel way better all of a sudden.

I couldn't help the grin pulling on my lips as the mental image of the sky over the stronghold filling with winged fury just made my day.

"You've been here the whole time?" Damn, I could have used them in so many scenarios, if I'd only known.

"Not at all," Max said. "We reside within the veils themselves."

Shock. Hang on, veils? And another memory, of being lost, drained of blood. Alone and dying.

His eyes didn't change, but Max nodded.

"The young maji would never have rescued you from the veil where you were trapped," he said, "if we hadn't opened the way for you."

Wow. "I guess I owe you a big thank you," I said, feeling my throat tighten. Guardian angels the size of a house? Sign me up.

"Not at all," he said. "It was our honor. And our duty to you and to Fate."

I guess I could forgive Fate for the past then, as long as it stayed out of my way from now on.

Yeah, that was going to happen.

"For now," Max said, body shrinking further until he was no bigger than Dad, gray skin taking on a pinker, more natural tone, though his corneas remained that same, shining diamond. "We have a rescue to undertake."

Meira. Damn it, where were my priorities?

Gasp. One further memory made my urgency even more abrupt.

"Quaid." My hands trembled violently a moment. "Trill and her brothers."

"Caught by the Brotherhood." I looked up, realized Max already knew.

"Can you help me free them, too?" That blow to my head really did a number, but frankly I wished someone would whack me again to make me forget I'd abandoned them.

To save Meira.

Still.

Max's eyes darkened, as though the light behind the jewel went out a moment. "We can try," he said.

Not the resounding "hell yeah" I was looking for, but he didn't say no. So I'd just let that be a yes and carry on.

"Enough yammer," I said, taking his hand again. "You driving or am I?"

Max's laugh went a long way to endearing him further. A dragon with a sense of humor and almost limitless creation power? We were going to be very good friends, I could just tell.

"Perhaps I should lead the way," he said. "Since you don't know where we're going."

Oh. Right.

I don't know what I was expecting. A chorus of angelic cherubs singing their hearts out. Fireworks and the stink of brimstone, maybe. Instead, Max simply tore a hole in the veil and stepped through.

Just like I would have done.

Not sure why knowing how similar we were freaked me out, but it did.

Yup yup.

Be ready, his mind touched mine, brushed against it, really. Even so, the briefest contact made me gasp as the vastness of his spirit opened for a moment and showed me his soul.

Good thing he stopped talking before he let us out the other end. Or I wouldn't have been able to function.

As it was, my temper saved me, as per usual. The second we passed through the veil into the dark beyond, I spotted Meira. Fighting. On the edge of a platform, so close my demon shrieked in fear and drove me forward to save her.

I might as well not have bothered. As it turned out, despite Max's knowledge to the contrary, Meira seemed to have this little battle well in hand. Her amber eyes flashed at me as she spun and planted her booted foot—platforms edged with six-inch spikes—into the chest of one of her kidnappers.

I tried not to wince at the sound of him screaming as he fell.

And fell.

And—

Thud.

Ick.

Another went down under a swift blow from Max's big fist as he roared. Not a normal roar, like one my demon might utter. Oh, no, not even close. His roar sounded like a freight train was coming. Sorry, ten freight trains. And an earthquake.

Meira's wide-eyed stare left her wide open to an attack, but I was there, lashing out with both fists, calling on my marital arts training and the pure fighting power of my demon, snapping her attacker's nose in crunch of splintering bone and then a solid thunk as my other fist impacted his breastbone, the deep, wet sound of his insides tearing almost enough to cool my temper.

Almost.

I spun to find Max had a demon pinned even as my sister flashed me a grin, long hair trailing around her in the breeze.

"Nice of you to show up," she said. I took a step toward her, hooked her with one hand, dragged her back from the edge. Only then did I answer.

"Way to get yourself kidnapped." I grinned back.

She shrugged. "I was bored. Needed a little excitement."

We stood there a long moment, giggling. It was only

Max's soft sigh that broke our hysterical moment.

"This one is their leader," he said.

Meira raised a perfectly arched eyebrow at me before nodding to him. "Good guess," she said.

"Meems, this is I can't pronounce his name so call him Max." I turned to the dragon who smiled at me. "Max, my sister, Princess Hathenemeira, heir to First Seat of Demonicon."

He bowed his head to her. "A great honor, Your Highness," he said. Hoisted the groaning demon in one hand as his head tilted, diamond eyes glittering. "What would you like me to do with this?"

Meira's answering grin was vicious. "I think he needs to meet my father," she said. "And say hello to the bitch who hired him."

I bumped her fist. "Time to narrow down Dad's choices."

Meira's anger glinted in her eyes. "Can't wait," she said.

chapter sixteen

Meira activated the lift, the elevator rising toward the top of the Seat. I tried not to look down, though the one glimpse I had was of a ragged shoreline and a vast expanse of black water. We had to be on the other side of the mountain from the Parade and Ostrogotho.

The platform came to a halt not quite at the top.

"This way," Meira said, stalking off on her giant boots, horns catching the light as she stomped her way down the polished stone corridor, torn robes flaring out behind her. I followed, Max beside me, the slowly rousing kidnapper in his hand. I glanced back over my shoulder at the other two unconscious demons still lying on the platform and almost asked Meira what she wanted to do about them.

Held my tongue. The mood she was in, they'd be following their friend over the edge. Besides, I had no doubt she would prefer to track them down at her leisure and show them just how disappointed she was in their behavior.

Hoped they knew how to run.

I'd clearly not done enough exploring of the Seat. I had no idea there was a back staircase up the rest of the way to the top. Filed the information away for later, just in case.

Meira slowed her pace just a little to make sure we kept stride as she hit the top and headed straight for Dad, sideways through the gathered court, family scattering with little shrieks of fear as my sister's power formed a sharp point and shoved them aside.

I stayed behind her, Max at my side, not wanting my presence to lessen Meira's show. Because, knowing my sister, she was about to put on one hell of a performance.

No way she'd let this go without the whole of Demonicon knowing.

Dad surged up from his throne, our grandfather doing the same as Meira burst into the center aisle and spun to face them. Her long, elaborate robe was torn in places, her normally perfect hair hanging from the large clasps holding her curls in place. But she didn't look unkempt to me—far from it. I fought more grinning at the sight of her going all Amazon on our father.

"Ruler!" Her voice echoed in the silence as everyone stared in shock. "I bring charges against Merlotsenilater."

A tall, handsome demon woman flinched, eyes flickering to me, to Max. To his burden. The moment she did, her red skin paled just as she inched sideway as if prepping for flight.

I don't think so.

My power snapped around her, jerked her into the aisle, where she fought and twisted inside a net of maji magic.

Dad sank into his seat again, brow pulled down over his amber eyes. "What have you done, Merlot?"

Meira didn't wait for the demon to answer. "I have only now won my freedom," she snarled, "from a band of kidnappers bent on my death." She spun, pointed one imperious finger at the wretch dangling from Max's hand. Though not much smaller than the drach, he was no match for my new friend's strength or the power suppressing the demon's magic. "This beast was their leader. You shall have the truth from him and no other."

Dad nodded, Demonicon's full power pressing forward as Max released the now cowering demon and squashed him tight in a fist-like grip. "You will confess," Dad said.

The demon groveled, face pressing to the stone floor. "The princess is right," he said. "Lady Merlotsenilater ordered myself and my companions to capture and kill Her Highness."

The demon woman froze, face contorting in fear.

"Haralthazar," she said, voice dripping what sweetness she could muster while my magic squeezed her so hard she could barely breathe. "My love."

Dad turned his head, waved in her direction.

"My daughter and heir," he said, voice low, empty, "take what is your right."

Meira poked me with her power.

My turn, she sent.

I released the suddenly sobbing demon, knowing what was coming, but unable to look away even though I wanted to. Yes, I was still furious at the woman for thinking she could kill my sister. But knowing what fate awaited her still gave me goosebumps.

Meira's power took my place. "You were always unworthy of him," she hissed.

Merlotsenilater's terror died as she snarled, her demon anger answering my sister's challenge. "I would have had him," she said, "if not for you."

Meira's vicious smile gave me chills. "Exactly," she said. And opened her power wide, devouring the other demon's magic to the dregs of her soul.

I was there, in Meira's mind, when the last of Merlotsenilater essence left her, came to my sister. When the monster of need rose inside Meira, fighting to be free, to take on more power, to turn and absorb all the magic in the room, to drain them all.

All.

She didn't really need me, but I was there for her anyway, my maji power steady, comforting as she fought down the curse of all demonkind, defeating the creature inside her once again, absorbing the last of Merlotsenilater's magic.

The demon woman's body fell, eyes empty, staring, her soul gone to my sister. I finally looked away as a pair of Guards marched forward and grasped her empty shell, lifting her up.

"To the volcano," my sister said. "And death."

They saluted with their free hands before spinning and carrying the silent and empty husk away.

From the terrified looks on two other demon women's faces, they had to be Things #2 and #3. I refused to give them any further attention past understanding they were all that stood between Mom and Dad getting back together.

Oh, and the fact my father was Ruler of Demonicon. Right. There was that, too.

Still.

Dad rose from his throne, power crackling around him as Henemordonin stood, my grandfather's amber eyes fixed in a tight frown on Max. The hard-nosed old demon had a tough enough time with new things. Couldn't wait to see what dear old Gramps thought of the fact I knew a dragon.

Snort.

"Court will now disperse," Dad said.

I could tell the gathered family was pissed, hoping for more excitement. Sure, they'd looked afraid earlier, but from the eagerness of their power, the way they whispered together and gawked at me and Max, they would have loved for the entertainment portion of this evening to go on longer.

Me? Not so much. I was tired, suddenly cranky and really just wanted to go home and hug my husband.

After rescuing Quaid and the Zornovs.

Was it wrong I wanted to hug Liam first?

We retreated, not to Dad's office, but to the lab under the Seat where I'd once returned Theridialis's soul to him after the battle over the Node. Sassafras's father turned to smile at us from where he hovered over an experiment, coming to hug me as my body shrank to human shape again now all the excitement was over.

He noticed, from the way his lips pursed like he wanted to ask a question, but Theridialis didn't comment. Oh, I'm sure he would have. Absolutely. Probably would have asked to study me or something creepy. But as he moved to speak, his eyes lifted and landed on someone over my shoulder.

And he froze, mouth hanging open.

I turned, shrugged. "What's the matter, Theridialis," I said. "Never seen a dragon before?"

Dad twitched, spinning toward the tall, diamond-eyed

figure while Henemordonin snorted, crossing his arms over his broad chest.

"You certainly have wild notions, granddaughter," he said. Like I needed the reminder. "*Apparantelo* are simply animals. While he, clearly, is not."

Eyeroll.

"And yet," Max said in his vibrating voice, shaking the room around us, "I am as she speaks, Henemordonin. Though the term is drach, Syd."

"Right." I snapped my fingers. "Sorry, forgot."

Meira laughed when the three demons just stared. "Thank you," she said to Max. "I didn't get a chance to say that earlier. Your help was most welcome."

Max bowed his head to her. "My great pleasure, Your Highness," he said.

"Now wait just one minute," Henemordonin began.

Didn't get to finish.

The air beside Max shimmered, the veil tearing just a little, a crack appearing. And, through it, shone the image of my grandmother. Ahbi's form shivered as she smiled at Max before scowling at my grandfather and shaking a finger. Her power reached out to me, hugged both myself and my sister before she sighed and the slice vanished in a flare of amber fire.

"There now," I said. "Since Ahbi herself seems to believe, I think any further conversation about Max's heritage is moot, don't you?"

That shut up my grandfather. Snap.

I know Theridialis would have pounced on Max with a gazillion questions and more tests for the drach than he could perform in ten lifetimes. Good thing the giant dragon in human form simply smiled at the scientist and shook his head.

"Perhaps another time," he said. "Fate awaits."

And my friends. I really had to go.

So much disappointment on a demon face I had never seen. Caught myself almost laughing—if it weren't for the growing fear and need to get back to the stronghold—even as a familiar figure appeared through the small doorway and eased his way toward us on silent feet. I smiled at Rameranselot as he waved to me with his own grin of welcome.

"Princess," he said. "Congratulations on your marriage."

Oh, yeah. Ram had been in the running there for a while, but we both knew he was the wrong choice. And, as he sidled up to my sister, and I saw how she looked at him, I realized just how happy I was he and I weren't together.

They made a very delicious couple.

"Thanks," I said. Turned to Max. "I hate to break up the party, but we have some asses to kick, do we not?"

He didn't smile this time. "I only know what Fate dictates," he said. "And so, I follow you, Sydlynn Hayle,

Light One."

There he went again, all formal and crap.

Whatever. I had a dragon on my side. And until Ameline managed to make it here and pick up hers, I had the advantage. Maybe I'd pay her a little visit.

Wondered if Max could breathe fire.

Heh.

Meira bent, kissed my cheek as I tore open the veil and turned to Dad.

"Listen," I said, crankies returning, "maybe you should reevaluate your mate choices at some point."

Dad sighed. "Nice to see you, cupcake."

Snarl.

I reached for Ahbi, ready to go back to the stronghold, drach in tow, and get my friends back. Realized the veil didn't show stone walls but the basement at home. Turned to frown at my sister.

Just in time to see her face go deathly pale as her body stiffened before collapsing to the floor.

CHAPTER SEVENTEEN

Zero hesitation.

Endless fury.

No doubt.

I dove through the veil after my sister's magic, my power already reaching out to squeeze the life from Ameline Benoit. Peripherally, I felt Max traveling with me, his magic humming through the veil with equal rage, the pair of us leaping out into my basement as I raised a hammer blow of maji power to crush the thieving bitch like a bug.

Only to pull up short at the fact she wasn't alone.

Not by a long shot.

Iepa stood beside her, face a mask of misery. My maji guide/backstabbing pain the tuckus hovered there, barely able to meet my gaze, her eyes brimming with tears. And that wasn't all, of course it wasn't. Ameline's own little fairy godfather, the dark maji Trinol, waited on her other side, night-black skin shining in the glow of Demonicon on the other side of the veil tear.

What. The. Freaking. Hell.

They weren't looking at me, neither of the maji. In fact, the moment I touched down, Iepa's tearful face flashed with hope while Trinol's showed fear. Both backed off a step as my big friend stepped out of the veil next to me, his power rippling with such anger I felt the house shake above me.

Didn't care. Not while Ameline smiled at me, Meira's magic hovering, fighting her, just outside my enemy's grasp.

I ignored the pounding of feet overhead coming our way, the flare of concerned family magic and the thrum of Sidhe raised by the disturbance of our arrival. I didn't have time to warn Shenka and Liam, or Sassafras, for that matter, as his demon power joined my second and husband on their way down the steps.

I had bigger issues to deal with. Like killing Ameline. I warned her, didn't I?

Couldn't wait.

Iepa's power reached for mine, a solid wall of maji magic holding me back as her misery returned.

"It must be this way," she said, voice thick with unshed tears.

My sympathy level for her poor me attitude went

about as far as the first layer of my bubbling temper.

"Save it," I snarled as Shenka skidded to a halt on the bottom step, Liam right behind her, both staring with huge eyes at the scene unfolding before them. Sassafras scampered forward, circling our little group, hissing at Ameline as I went on. "Your little show and betrayal has gone far enough."

Iepa opened her mouth to respond.

And Max roared. So. Loud. My teeth rattled together. No, wait. My bones did, too. And the entire house shook so violently from the sound I felt the family magic struggle to keep it on the foundation.

"It does not have to be this way," Max said as my ears cleared from ringing. "And you know it. A choice of power source from the demon realm can be made instead."

I wanted to high five him before flipping both maji the finger, but chose instead to grasp my sister's power from Ameline's grip and rip her free.

Ameline let go after a short struggle. She might have been close to complete, but she was still no match for me, not with a battling demon soul fighting her every step of the way. Meira's magic hovered next to me a moment before I sent her back through the veil and to her body.

Okay, now I could kill the bitch.

Wicked.

"You idiot!" Ameline's temper rarely showed, but

when it did, it showed. Flares of fire erupted from her body, cascading sparks to the concrete floor and the pentagram etched on the surface. "I need that power to be your equal." That had to hurt. Hoped so. "Do you want the Brotherhood to win? Is that it?"

Snarl, grumble, growl.

"Sydlynn," Iepa said, desperation in her voice. "Time is so short. You must allow it."

No. Way. "Not Meems," I said. "You keep your filthy hands off my sister."

Ameline crossed her arms over her chest, hate blazing from her ice blue eyes. "Unless you have an alternative," she said, "I suggest you get over your weakness about your family," she used the word like a curse, "and allow me to do what I need to."

Uh-huh, not a chance in hell freezing over.

I glanced sideways at Max, saw his anger receding. Knew if I lost his backing, Meems was done for.

He turned his head, diamond eyes meeting mine. "There is another way," he said. And spun on his heel, power reaching for the still-glowing tear in the veil, the scene on the other side holding my attention a moment as Dad shouted silently, Theridialis bent over my sister who now shook her head as she struggled to rise.

It was only then I felt Ahbi watching, listening, understood as Max's musical language poured out of him and toward my demon grandmother what he had in mind.

Felt Ahbi's surging acceptance in answer.

She slipped free of the edge, as though the Node chose to release her, the veil snapping shut behind her just as Meira reached toward me, fear on her face. So strange to see Ahbi hovering there, alone, a glowing shape of towering power, curved horns and fiery eyes. My grandmother's spirit smiled at me before turning and slamming her full presence into Ameline.

The dark maji gasped, staggering back, her body engulfed in amber flames. I watched my grandmother kick her ass from the inside before Ahbi settled down, one final flare of her appearing in Ameline's eyes before my enemy pulled herself upright, panting for breath.

Her lips curved in a vicious grin. "At last," she said, voice full of power, her maji magic appearing in a rippling rainbow around her. "At last!"

I rolled my eyes, fully expecting a resounding mwahahaha evil laugh, even as I saw Ahbi flex herself again, Ameline gasping, the maji net falling apart as she fought for control.

I smirked at her struggles. Ameline might be whole, but there was no way my demon grandmother was going to make it easy for her. And I had no doubt, once our little venture into Brotherhood territory was over, Ahbi would be doing everything she could to part ways with Ameline.

Wait. Damn it. I couldn't fight the Brotherhood now.

Quaid.

And Trill and company. Damn it, Syd. Not just him.

I turned and tore open the veil, reached for my sister, needing at least that reassurance.

You're okay? I felt her, caught a glimpse of Ram supporting her while Dad and Henemordonin argued in the background.

Fine, she sent. *Thanks for the help. I had no idea she was so strong.*

She's not, I sent, letting her feel my anger. *She had help.*

And now, so do you. Meira hugged me mentally. *I don't feel Ahbi.*

She's safe and sound with Ameline. I laughed evilly and my sister joined me.

I hope she burns her to a cinder, Meira sent. Sobered. *You be safe.*

I will, I sent. *Love you.*

I let the veil seal shut again, so odd without my grandmother's touch to it, spun back.

Ameline glared at me, lips curling back from her gleaming white teeth. "It's time," she said.

Crappy craplick on a crapstick. I felt my stomach sink into my feet. "You have them all now." Of course she did. I knew that.

"With your other grandmother's power inside me," she said, "I am complete."

The taint from Pannera. Her new soul fed by the lost

ones of the Sidhe. All the power she stole from Belaisle to feed her sorcery. Gram's witch magic. And her maji power, honed on her use of blood magic.

Equal to me at last.

CHAPTER EIGHTEEN

Was it wrong I felt suddenly stunned, as though someone hit me on the head again?

"Is it time, then?" I met Iepa's eyes, stunned to think this could be over very soon. Which meant rescuing Quaid and the Zornovs would have to wait.

But every minute ticking by with them in Belaisle's hands could mean their death. Maybe not Trill and her brothers, not if he thought he needed them. But Quaid was a liability.

Yes, I worried about him. A lot. Sue me for still caring.

The quick shake of Iepa's head, her glance sideways at Trinol, unclenched the knot in my gut a fraction. "Not yet," she said. "There is still another to find before the prophecy can be complete."

Cool. Enough time to make the daring rescue so I

could focus.

Ameline spun on the two maji, her anger flaring once again. Made me wonder how much influence Ahbi had over her and if it was my grandmother's temper showing.

"Prophecy." She spit the word at them both, magic swirling around her. "I am the Dark One and I will fulfill my destiny in the way of my choosing."

Iepa was already reaching for her, Trinol's low cry and deep scowl marring his flawless skin as Ameline's form flared with iridescent light and vanished.

The dark maji guide's snarl of fury came only a moment before he, too, flashed with power and disappeared, leaving Iepa to stare after them with both hands over her mouth.

"Sydlynn," she whispered in a voice full of horror. "You must go after her."

Not. "You're so worried about Ameline," I said, "you do it. I'm tired of cleaning up after you."

Max snorted softly beside me as I turned away from the shaking maji and scooped up my demon cat. His amber eyes flared as his tail thrashed against me.

Liam and Shenka joined us, Charlotte appearing behind them, only now visible as she descended to my side.

"Please, Sydlynn." Iepa didn't approach, just stood there and trembled, hands outstretched toward me. "Before it's too late."

"I've done everything you've asked of me," I said. "And you've done nothing but betray me at every turn." Okay, not every turn. But she wasn't all that much help, damn it, and I was tired of being her lackey girl. "I have real friends to save. Who mean far more to me than Ameline Benoit could ever hope to."

"It's not my choice," Iepa wailed. "Nor is it yours. Fate, your Fate, ours, dictates. We are all just Her tools."

I rested my chin on Sassy's head as I scowled at her. "You're saying Fate is a person now?"

Max rumbled an agreement before Iepa could answer. "Yes, indeed," he said. "Both the Light and the Dark have a Fate they answer to, Syd." He glared at my maji guide. "You did not tell her so?"

Iepa didn't respond, hanging her head.

"Irresponsible and pathetic," he snarled at her. "And you hope for Light to win? How? By making your vessel guess at every turn?"

"Fate wanted—"

He cut her off with a deep growl and a puff of fire from his lips. Guess that answered my question about the whole flame breathing thing. "I know Fate far better than you," he said. "And she would never, ever ask such a thing." Max turned his back on Iepa. "But one thing is certain." I wasn't going to like what he had to say. Positive of it. "You must go after Ameline. Without her, you are lost and only the gathered armies of the magic races will stand against the Brotherhood."

And lose. Yeah, watched that movie a few times, thanks.

Liam's arm went around my shoulders. "I think you've all bullied her enough, haven't you?"

So sweet. Misguided and unnecessary. But that was my Liam.

"Sydlynn," Iepa's tears trickled over her cheeks as she trembled. "I beg you, you must not allow her to die."

"She's not immortal?" I was, supposedly. And pretty much invincible.

"You both have your strengths and weaknesses," Iepa said. "Your immortality is not shared between you."

Which made me wonder what I had she didn't. Like it mattered.

Damn Ameline anyway. And my sense of duty.

Sucked.

"Syd," Sass said, one paw rising to touch my cheek as I looked down at him. "Don't let everything you've been through be for nothing."

Shenka's power bumped against me. "You can kill her yourself later," she said.

Charlotte's growl of agreement made me smile. "I'll hold her down," the weregirl said. "But you've come so far. We all have, thanks to you. Don't let this fall apart because of her selfishness."

And that was what it came down to, didn't it?

Ameline and her stupid ego.

"Fine," I said. Handed Sass to Liam. Stood on my tiptoes to kiss my husband. His hand dove into my hair, pulled my mouth tight against his, a thread of fear passing through the love and support he sent me.

"Love you," he whispered. "Please come back to me."

Choke. I turned away, couldn't afford the weakness I felt at leaving him behind. Leaving them all behind.

I looked up into Max's diamond eyes as he smiled and nodded.

"Let me take you to her," he said. "I think it's time the Brotherhood understood just who they are up against."

Maybe we could kill two birds with one dragon. After all, Ameline had to have gone to the stronghold plane, right? Sudden relief almost made my knees wobble. Rescue Quaid and the Zornovs, scoop up Ameline and we'd be good to go.

"No," Iepa said in a gasp of breath. "You cannot interfere, drach."

He glared at her, a puff of smoke emerging from his flaring nostrils.

"Go back to minding your own business, child," he said as he seized my hand.

I didn't get a chance to ask him what he was talking about, what kind of show he had in mind. The moment he was done putting Iepa in her place, he tore open the veil and dragged me through.

Until his body morphed, changed beside me just after he tossed me over his head. The veil's rubber membrane didn't slow me down as I seemed to rise forever, heart pounding, not afraid of heights inside the veil itself.

Opened my mouth to scream as I exited the other end in an empty, gray sky and started to fall.

CHAPTER NINETEEN

I thudded, breathless, into a hard, dark shape as Max, in drach form, swooped beneath me, banking to catch me across his broad back.

My swearing was lost in the rush of wind, but I have no doubt from the rumbling chuckle rising from his warm, scaled body he found it amusing when I explained to him just how furious I was to be dumped out and left to fall to my death.

And then there was no time for talking, or no breath for it at least, as he caught a thermal current and my stomach rose to my throat as I floated, weightless a moment, over the wide, emptiness of the barren landscape below.

Shudder. Just. Shudder.

And yet, lying there on his back, clinging on to the hard edges of his scales for dear life, as I looked out over the plane, I had to admit to myself this was the coolest freaking thing I'd ever done. Witches didn't fly, not in airplanes. Just in case our magic interfered with something important and made the aircraft plunge to fiery doom. And with my fear of heights, I never imagined I'd enjoy soaring.

Almost shattered my vertigo completely.

The stronghold stretched out to my right, massive, more so than I expected, covering a giant plot of ground. There had to be places in it no one explored, it was so vast. The plane itself seemed to go on forever, a vast expanse of nothing. No trees, shrubs, green, mountains, water... just gray and dead land and a gray and empty sky.

Whatever happened here, why this place seemed lifeless, I had no doubt the Brotherhood had a hand in its death.

The weight of Max's mind on mine told me my sightseeing was over.

There, he sent.

I looked where he turned, banking his massive form over the flat plain, one broad sweep of his wings carrying us toward the huge stone stronghold. His eyes were way better than mine, obviously, but it didn't take long for my demon sight, and his distance crushing flight, to show me what he saw.

A tiny figure ran across the emptiness, pursued by a river of ants. Or, at least that's what they looked like from up—

Gulp. My phobia returned in a rush of terror, chest tight, stomach a fist of agony, blood freezing in my veins—

You must help her, Max sent, cutting through my panic. *Syd, I need to focus on the Brotherhood.*

Right. Double cheek smack. Onward.

Wind rushed around me, pushing against me, trying to scoop me from Max's back. I anchored myself with power, feeling his energy embrace Shaylee as her Sidhe earth magic dug deep and locked me in place.

Still nervous, feeling hysterical giggles rising, I sat up, legs stretched uncomfortably to straddle his back. This was no horse, but a massive dragon I rode, and I finally had to just trust my Sidhe power and cross my legs in front of me.

Held firm by a cushion of earth power, confidence rising, I left Shaylee to handle our safety and reached for Ameline. And it was her, running toward us, as we flew toward her, Max swooping to the ground, rushing forward until I could see the brightness of her eyes.

My demon's power latched on, heaved her onto Max's shoulder as we skimmed over the furious Brotherhood sorcerers. Black balls of empty beat against his underside and I felt the drach shudder even as the massive down sweep of his wings carried us up again.

I peered over his back, saw the sorcerers fall,

sprawled by the thrust of wind his wings created, their attack cut off as he threw himself into the air and far above their reach.

The veil tore, Max turning sideways to hurtle through the gap just as it snapped shut behind his tail.

No! I shouted into the veil. *Go back!*

I could still feel him, the anchor Shaylee created holding firm.

We cannot, he sent. *Syd, the time is at hand. Your friends will have to wait.*

My argument died in a bout of gasping and clutching at him as the veil opened one more time and he zoomed out, still sideways.

Oh. My. Swearword.

If you don't straighten up, I sent, *I'm going to kick your drach ass.*

Another chuckle, this one with a hint of wickedness. *You'll never be free of your fear*, he sent, *unless you face it and defeat it. Besides*, his wings beat once as he righted himself before dipping down to the familiar bowl-like peak under the Demonicon sky, *I would never let you fall.*

Says you, I sent even as my temper flared. *I'm going back, with or without you.*

His huge head swung around, diamond eye glittering.

If you go back, he sent, *without her, without the fourth, you will die and this will all have been for nothing.*

You don't know that, I sent. Wanted to call him a liar.

Doubted myself too much to do so.

Syd, he sent. *Please believe Fate works in ways none of us can comprehend. And, if it is meant to happen, your friends will survive.*

That didn't sound hopeful.

I gathered my power, reached for the veil. To hell with him and Fate. I couldn't leave them to suffer.

Felt his swell around me, hold me tight.

I will do everything in my power to stop you, he sent. *Just as I will do everything in my power to help you succeed against the Brotherhood. Please, trust Fate. There has to be a reason your friends are trapped there.*

Easy for him to say.

And we will be there again soon, he sent. *For the final battle. Which feels closer than I have ever felt it. We can find them then, when this is over.*

Too late. What if we were too late? A storm of self-loathing and frustration swirled in my gut, poking me with fear, anger, the desperate need to help them.

And yet.

Why did it feel like he was right?

Fine, I snapped. *But if anything happens to them, I'm holding you responsible.*

If that makes you feel better, he sent.

Didn't. Not even a little bit.

I glanced over, noticed Ameline still struggling to hold on. Didn't offer to help.

She was maji now, too, wasn't she? I was done with

handholding. And rescuing, thanks.

The drach waited for us, watching as Max landed, the backwash of his wing strokes sending a soft mist of dust into the air as his back legs settled onto the black stone before his front end joined them.

Smooth, precise landing. Thank you for flying Drach Air.

Ameline leaped free, her fury snapping and crackling around her as she glared up at me. Wow, Ahbi was really doing a number on her. I hadn't seen so much emotion from the dark maji ever.

"Why didn't you come with me?" Her magic thrashed against mine, but never made contact. Max's growl followed a puff of smoke, the glow of flame showing around his long, narrow muzzle while his power flowed outward to block her. "This could have been over if you had just come with me."

Max morphed as he spoke, going from looming drach to huge man in a few breaths. "Don't be a fool, Dark One," he said while his people hummed in agreement. "The prophecy—the Fates—are very specific. Not even we are outside their purview."

That was interesting. "I thought you were random?"

He shrugged, smiled. "Is there really such a thing, Syd? Or is random merely another term for a choice to be made?"

No time for philosophical discussions. Not with

Ameline still blowing steam.

Max returned his attention to her. "There is much to happen between now and the time of your battle," he said. "Did you really think Fate would allow you to break the threads they created? That you, little maji, are more important than the prophecy itself?"

Zing. I liked him more and more as time went on, uh-huh. Even if he was between me and Quaid.

And the Zornovs, Syd.

Ameline's sullen scowl was her only answer.

"We have an appointment to keep," the female drach stepped forward again. The one who said she was for Ameline. I tried not to hold it against her.

"Two of them," Max agreed as I silently labeled the female Mabel.

What? Not like I could pronounce her name either, likely.

Ameline looked her up and down with an air of disdain while I shook my head and poked her with power. She snarled at me while I turned to Max.

"Is this the one we needed?"

He shook his head, diamond eyes cold and quiet. "No," he said. "Only Fate knows the identity of the one who must join you."

"Two maji," Mabel said while the song of the drach grew in volume and layered texture of harmony. I wished I had a recorder, some way to capture it. Now that I wasn't afraid and on edge about Meira, it was really beautiful.

"Two sorcerers." Max said.

"One of the Light and one of the Dark." Mabel nodded to Ameline who narrowed her eyes. I could see her mind churning even as my own spun circles.

"Does that mean Ameline is going to fight for the Brotherhood?" Just like her to turn to the bad guys at the end.

Just kill her now, my demon sent. *We'll sort it out later.*

"Only one can tell you what you need to know," Max said while Ameline's power snapped at me. He turned to her then. "And only one can share what knowledge you require."

Mabel reached out and set her hand on Ameline's shoulder.

"Come," she said. "It is time."

For?

I took Max's hand as Ameline shrugged free of Mabel's touch.

His diamond eyes blinked slowly, once.

"You must speak to Fate," he said.

chapter twenty

I was in the veil before I could gulp down that particular tidbit, but had absorbed it by the time Max opened the other side and I stepped out into Center. I knew it immediately, felt the familiar pull of longing, as we stood on the edge of the great city that was the home of the maji.

A soft sigh escaped me. Yes, I'd left here last time pissed off and ready for a fight, but that didn't mean its effect on me had gone away. Now my anger was cooled, my focus on finding what I needed to know to move forward, the call of Center and the peace it offered my soul was almost too much to bear.

Until I caught Ameline smirking at me as if she knew what I was feeling.

Screw her. And the stupid spell this place had over me. When this was done, I couldn't wait to go home to my family and never see Center again.

New resolve in place, I marched ahead of the others, past the soaring fountains and through the beautiful streets, ignoring the watching eyes of the maji as I grew in size at the foot of the massive stairs until I could walk up them and into the huge building.

And found Zeon standing at the top, waiting for me, a sweet smile on his Santa Claus face.

"Sydlynn," he said, warmth radiating from him, kindness and calm. Peace, the peace of Center. "We are so happy to see you return, my daughter."

Oh *hell* no. I pushed against him with my full maji power, felt his shell of false joviality crack, the quivering fear he hid behind it peeking through.

"Careful, Zeon," I said as his power rippled around him in an attempt to seal the gap. "Your old-fashioned notions are showing."

At least he dropped the act, lips falling into a frown as Iepa appeared behind him. She looked relieved, not that I cared, as her leader's magic pushed back against me.

Only to have Max and Mabel take their turn.

Zeon's face paled, ghostly and gray as he staggered back a step. "What have you done?" His eyes fixed on first one, then the other, drach. "Why are you here?"

"You know why," Max said, climbing the last step, towering over Zeon. "She must speak to Fate. And you will not stand in her way any longer, maji."

Zeon shuddered, shaking his head, eyes wild. "It cannot be," he said. "She must find her own way."

"According to whom?" Max's voice vibrated the very steps beneath my feet, the trembling making Zeon's large belly shake, his bearded jowls shiver. "You are not the keeper of Fate, Zeon. She is her own master."

I felt him try to push Max back, knew the instant he caved as his old head bowed.

"You will be the ruin of everything, drach," Zeon said.

"Old fool," Max said, moving him aside with one massive hand, "you've almost done that job for me."

I followed my dragon friend past the sorrowful Zeon, wondering now how much of the old maji's attitude was act and how much real. Didn't matter, not now.

Why doesn't he want us here? Surely, he had to see the signs of what was coming.

The maji of light have always believed Fate must be uncovered, Max sent. *While the maji of the dark believe Fate must be shown the way.*

I know it's late in the game, I sent, *but maybe I could switch sides?*

His chuckle eased my mind. *I'm happy to have you on the side of light, thank you,* he sent. *Zeon and his people will no longer stand in your way. Forgive Iepa, if you can. She has been working under difficult circumstances, controlled by the dictates of her people. And yet, she has managed to guide you despite them. A massive feat.*

I grumbled at him silently. *We'll see*, I sent.

Charitable of me, I know. But in for a penny, throw the baby out with the bathwater.

Okay, some mixed metaphors didn't work, even for me, but I was running on fumes.

Something stirred around me, inside me, a feeling of rightness as I walked the cold, white halls of the large building, ceiling arching open above me, blue sky bright. A lightness took over, fear fading, urgency, until I found peace at last.

But not fed by the power of Center. This peace, this quiet of my soul, came from another place. From the presence of whoever sat at the edge of the pool at the end of the building.

My companions stopped, stayed behind as I moved on. I heard Ameline arguing with Mabel, but ignored her, all of my focus, my entire being, locked on the sweet-faced young woman splashing her toes in the sparkling water. She looked up as I neared, the most amazing smile I'd ever seen shining on her face.

From her empty, white eyes.

"Sydlynn," she said. "Oh, my very dear. I've been waiting for you."

I sank to the edge of the fountain beside her, heart fluttering with so many emotions I didn't know what to say, what to do.

Blurted, as usual. "You're blind." Kicked myself for being such an idiot.

But she laughed and nodded, leaning forward to pat my hand. Her skin felt cool, soft, but not unusual and, despite the fact I could feel her maji power, there seemed to be nothing odd about her.

And everything. Everything.

"You have questions," she said, spinning to face me, empty eyes somehow fixed on me. "They've kept you from me, but I knew you would find the drach. That you would make your way here in time."

"How?" I didn't know, not even that she existed.

She laughed, a tinkling sound like tiny bells. "Silly," she said. "He told you, the one you call Max." Her nose wrinkled. "I like it, the name you chose for him."

Told me...?

"I'm Fate," she said. "I know everything."

My mind tried to shy sideways, but her magic held me softly in place as I struggled with the concept. Fought against the truth. No way. No. Way. I had choices, I really did. She didn't control me. And yet, finally, I sagged and accepted as her magic hugged me gently before letting me go.

"My brother and I," she said, "were born together, like this. Fates. He of the Dark and I of the Light. The first of the maji, after the drach were brought into being."

I nodded. Nothing else to do but listen.

She patted my hand again, fingers tracing over my rings. "I can't tell you how very proud I am," she said, cheeks pink as she blushed, though from happiness. I felt it in her and found myself flushing in answer. "You have done so well, come so far, exactly as you were meant to, despite—and because of—the maji's rules against assisting you. And now, your first task is at hand."

Um, what? "First?"

A trace of sadness flowed over her face. "I'm sorry," she said. "You have so much more to do, Syd. I wish I could lay the burden on another, but you were made for this. You understand? The unique circumstances of your birth, your development, your gathering of power, all were designed to bring you here, to me, now."

A sob built in my chest as my mind spun out centuries of hardship and loss. "Can I say no?" A stupid question.

But she smiled and nodded, leaning forward to kiss my cheek with unerring accuracy. "You can," she said. "It has always been up to you to choose. But your destiny leads you to only one path. Leaving that path is impossible for you now." Fate sat back, sighed. "My dear," she said, "you tell me now and you can go. I won't stop you, my visions will be rewritten, though I fear the outcome." She shook her head, blonde hair woven through with white blossoms so long the bottom floated in the water beside her. "Will you do as you are meant to save us all?"

Funny how I didn't hesitate, though my heart hung heavy inside me.

"Of course I will," I said, feeling her power embrace me tighter.

"I knew you would," she said. "You have been created from the most powerful of witches, demons, a vampire essence, carry the soul of a Sidhe princess. Your sorcery knows no equal, not even that of your Dark nemesis." Interesting. "And your creation power will be the Light we need to follow if the planes are to survive this coming conflict." She wove a soft ball of magic before her, pressing it into my chest. "Time itself has done her part to create you, Sydlynn Hayle. And you are perfect."

Nice of her to think so.

Now if only I believed it.

Fate drew me closer by her grip on my hand, lips against my ear. "Listen carefully. The battle you foresaw, the one Iepa showed you, came from Fate. But not from me."

The other Fate, then?

"The battle I see is far different," she said. "The prophecy is mine and mine alone. His visions would have you lose."

Well that sucked.

"His will take over if you fail. Even now, the

Brotherhood gather to hunt the magic races in a show of force the likes of which the planes have never seen. They draw power from the empty plane, from the gateways to the Universe through the stronghold."

Hang on, what did that mean?

"If you are willing," she went on before I could ask, "there will only be four in the end." I nodded, knew that much already. "You, the dark maji Ameline. Liander Belaisle of the Brotherhood."

And?

"You know the fourth already," she said. "And you must trust him no matter his mental state."

Holy. Was she talking about—

"Demetrius Strong fights for the Light with you," Fate said. "And he holds the final key to victory."

chapter twenty one

"You know he's nuts, right?" Yes, I'd learned to trust Demetrius, but holy. This was life and death of all planes stuff.

"His burdens are necessary," Fate said with sadness in her voice. "Everything has been, for both of you. You weren't able to kill Belaisle when you had him trapped with the oracles, because he is necessary." Oracles? Was he talking about the woman under the rainbow glass? "This fight will decide the course of Fate. Above all else, if you remember nothing I tell you or show you, trust Demetrius. Even when it goes against your heart to do so."

"What happens if we win?" Might be nice to have some advanced knowledge.

She shook her head, looking away, empty eyes on the water of the fountain. "The visions are dim," she said. "I can't see clearly past the battle." Why did I get the impression she wasn't being totally honest with me? Or maybe I was just paranoid.

Naw. Trusting my instincts on this one.

Fate's hand squeezed as her power swelled. "You don't believe," she said. "Will you see with me?"

I barely nodded in answer, realizing doing so was useless to her, only to be drawn in to a vision so powerful I stood there and watched as though it were happening right now.

Was able to see myself, Ameline. Belaisle and Demetrius on the empty plane. Alison was there, Mia. Rupe, my old friend turned enemy. The Zornovs and Quaid. Alive. Which lifted a massive burden from my shoulders.

They would be okay.

And then, in awe, as the sky filled with drach and the Brotherhood fought them.

And then, darkness.

I caught a brief flicker of something past the dark, but Fate cut me off before I could explore it, though I knew the location, the Sidhe cavern.

What wasn't she showing me?

"What happens during your fight will decide where time and destiny run from there. Yes, there are possibilities, but they are fuzzy, insubstantial." Fate released my hand. "But at that moment, when you face

Belaisle, everything, every plane, will stand still and even time will wait for the outcome."

Freaky. No pressure or anything.

I carefully shunted the giant, overwhelming terror stirring in my stomach into a tightly sealed box in the depths of my mind and did my best to leave it there. Worry wouldn't help, neither would big picture. One step at a time, one foot in front of the other.

Breathing wasn't optional.

Fate hugged me, brushing her lips over my forehead. "Thank you," she whispered, "for all of your sacrifice for those you love, for strangers and races you have never met. Terrible days are behind and even more hardship lies ahead." She hesitated before going on. "And I am so sorry for your loss. But please believe it has all been necessary, no matter what you might think of me and my task."

She might as well have punched me in the stomach. "What are you talking about?" Was someone going to die? Mom? Dad? Meems?

The image of an old lady with wispy hair and bare feet sitting in a sunbeam crossed my mind. Gram. No. But she was the logical choice, wasn't she? Weak, frail.

And if I lost her, I would die.

I felt Max approach, had to force air into my lungs as I reminded myself about the whole breathing thing again. I tried to convince myself she must have been talking about loss I'd already suffered.

Choke.

Even as my mind went back to Gram.

"My darling," Fate spoke to Max while terror tore a massive hole through me. "Your task awaits. You know what to do?"

I turned, heart pounding, to see my drach friend's shoulders sag, his head bowing.

"I do," he said. "And I am ready, no matter the consequences."

Was *he* going to die?

Why the hell did she have to say that? Now I was worried about every single person in my life.

Gram.

Please, no. Not Gram, Please.

He bowed to Fate, held out his hand to me. Mind whirling in a tornado of fear and doubt, I took it.

"Be well, my love," Fate said.

It took me a moment to realize she wasn't talking to me. But only after I registered the shining tears tracking down Max's cheeks.

I just wished I had the presence of mind to comfort him. Kind of hard to do when I was busy being terrified for the people I loved.

chapter twenty two

Ameline's unhappy scowl actually helped, pricking my temper and making my egos all surge in anger. A nice change from the spinning fear we all fell into after Fate's little "loss" pronouncement.

"Took long enough," she said before turning her back on me, confronting Mabel. "I take it my turn is coming sometime in the near future?"

Her ass was right there in front of me, beneath the black cloak she wore. One swift kick—

Do it, my demon snarled.

Use earth magic, Shaylee sent.

Temper, temper, my vampire's calm voice finished with, *don't miss*.

If only.

"Travel safely." I turned, surprised to find Fate standing behind us, empty eyes on Ameline. "Listen carefully to what my brother has to tell you, Dark Child. Your Fate will lead you where you need to go."

Ameline didn't turn, shoulders stiff, and the Light Fate sighed. Waved to me.

I wanted to ask her, to drill her for information, but there wasn't time. Only the horrible knowledge someone I loved was going to be lost to me.

That doesn't have to mean death, does it? My demon's heat cooled as she coiled, unhappy, inside me. *Not necessarily.*

Perhaps it just means someone is moving on? Shaylee's hint of hope did little to make me feel better.

You are immortal, my vampire sent. *Those around you are not. You must prepare yourself for the inevitable.*

Sigh.

Max's hand closed around mine as Mabel opened the veil this time, not even bothering to travel outside the city first. I spotted Iepa watching, hands clutched to her chest, but refused to answer her sad little smile.

Told myself there wasn't time as Max and I followed Mabel and Ameline through the gap in the veil.

Liar.

Why was I not surprised to step out of the other side and into darkness? Really, could they have been a bit more predictable? And while, yes, the city stretching out before me down the path was stunning in the night, sparkling with multi-hued lights, I caught myself heaving a reflexive sigh.

Max's smile shone in the dark. "They call it Core," he said, laughter in his voice.

Of course they did.

Posers, all of them. Kids who refused to play nice together, to share a sandbox. Seriously.

I hated the fact some of the most powerful beings in all the planes were way less grown up than I was.

Not promising.

Trinol waited for us at the entry to the city, black skin almost lost in the night.

"Welcome," he said. Stepped aside.

I let Ameline and Mabel take the lead, hanging back a little with Max. Nervous. Just in case I wasn't welcome. These were the dark maji, after all. Surely, they'd be unhappy about me showing up to rain on their little parade.

How startling to discover the contrary was true. The maji of this city seemed as interested in me being there as those of Center did about Ameline. And when we reached the center of the city, forced to grow and expand once again to climb identical stairs to an identical building, this one's columns and walls of jet marble, I found the leader of this place had a smile of greeting for me.

"I am Yosha," she said. "Be welcome here, those of the prophecy."

Huh. Nice. Zeon needed to take notes. I bowed my

head to her as Max let me go.

Ameline didn't bother, pushing past the dark maji woman. "Where is he?"

Thunder boomed, a lightning strike creating a flare of white. My insides shuddered from the aftereffect of the change in air pressure as a massive voice echoed above us.

"Ameline," the voice said, fury in his tone, "come to me."

Whoops. I grinned at her before making a moue of fake concern she seemed to be in trouble.

I really didn't think the rude hand gesture she flashed me in answer was called for.

So childish.

Snort.

No way I was being left behind, though. I followed her into the building, Max and Mabel keeping pace, the maji leader remaining behind. It wasn't long before I spotted the other Fate sitting next to a roaring fire. Max's hand on my shoulder held me back as Mabel turned with her hands folded in front of her, like some drach bodyguard.

"We must remain," Max said.

Grumble, mumble. But fair enough, I supposed.

Still, after what Fate told me, it would have been nice to eavesdrop. But no amount of poking and prodding made it past Mabel's guardian magic so I gave up and crossed my arms to wait.

My foot wouldn't stop tapping in anxious irritation. Pacing didn't help much, either. Was I really gone this long? It felt like a few minutes I talked with Fate. Ameline's little chat was freaking endless.

Needing a distraction, I turned on Max. "Mind telling me what the whole love thing was about?"

Syd. Sheesh. Tactful.

He flinched a little, but didn't back down. "My people were first," he said. "And I am first of my people."

Wow. Okay.

"Fate was next," he said, "and I have loved her since."

Tears rushed to the surface, a choking sob escaping me. Already on a tightrope with my own worries and emotions, that simple statement almost broke me for some reason. I reached out, squeezed his hand, let my magic flow to him, allowed him to feel my regret, my sadness for him.

His answered with gentle sorrow, as ancient as the planes themselves.

"You can never be together." Wow, I thought my life sucked.

He shook his head.

My sorrow retreated even as a zing of understanding almost made me gasp.

Syd, girl. You're holding hands with the oldest living

creature ever.

Holy.

I was so wrapped up in the knowledge of Max's reality I almost forgot what I was really waiting for. So when Ameline appeared, speculation etched in her features, I had to jerk myself back to the task at hand.

She'd definitely lost her flat emotionlessness, and I, for one, was glad. Considering I had a hard time not showing every single thing I felt on my face and in the way I carried my body, it was gratifying to know even the ice queen could be human.

The young man she'd spoken to joined us, identical to his sister Fate, though his hair was shaved to a soft stubble and his voice deeper than hers when he spoke.

"My friend," he addressed Max. "Love of my sister. It is good to see you again."

Max bowed to Fate. "And you."

Fate's face took on a hint of sorrow as he spoke again. "You understand your part? You will fulfill your task at the appointed time?"

Max nodded. "I am ready," he said.

I really would have loved to know what that was all about.

No time. Not for anything anymore.

"Be well," Fate said. "The moment of prophecy is nigh." He waved to me, then to Ameline. "The Dark and the Light are well met."

If he said so.

Max's hand on my shoulder was all the warning I had. One last look around Core and we were in the veil, while my nerves woke up and gave me a nice double-tap to my ribcage.

Game on.

Time to kick some Brotherhood ass once and for all.

I hoped.

chapter twenty three

I half expected to land in the empty plane right then and there, wind knocked out of me in a deep exhale of relief as Max delivered us into the basement of my house. Not that I wasn't up for the challenge or anything—sure, Syd, keep telling yourself so—the sight of Mom standing there, waiting for me, was almost enough to bring me to tears.

Almost? Okay, so a few were involved, but I hid them in her hair when I stepped forward and into her arms.

She held me a long moment, a solid rock, my rock, not speaking, her power saying everything she needed to say. When I finally pulled away, I felt more stable, less likely to fly apart, everything Fate told me kind of hitting me in one big blow.

But yeah. I could take it. Just watch me.

Intros all around, Mom didn't miss a beat, welcoming

the drach to our plane, even graciously ignoring Ameline. Instead of, you know, beating her to an undignified pulp. Mom amazed me with her restraint.

"Anything we can do to help," Mom said, turning to me, power blazing as the Council's magic answered. "The witch nation stands ready."

Oh boy, exactly what we didn't need. Hadn't Fate told me her brother's version was the one where everyone died and the planes blew up? Ameline's version. She couldn't have it. Not going to happen on my watch.

And if I fell, well... I wouldn't be around to see it end, would I?

"I need you to stay out of it," I said as Mom's shoulders tensed, face hardening in stubborn rejection. How did I know where her mind went? Because I knew exactly how I'd feel if she told me to keep calm and carry on. "Mom, I need you to watch over the family. And this plane." Felt my own tension mount as she frowned. "Under no circumstances are you to assemble an army and come after me."

Her blue eyes flared with fire before she finally nodded, anxiousness easing. "How did you know?" She shook her head. "I've been in touch with all the Councils. We've been quietly assembling as many Enforcers as we can in preparation for an assault."

Just like the visions Iepa showed me predicted. "Mom, you have to trust me," I said. Heard Ameline snort in derision behind me. Wanted to smack her even as I kept my focus on Mom. "This is my job. Mine and Ameline's. Liander Belaisle's." I paused, drew a breath. "And Demetrius Strong's."

Mom's eyes flew wide, mouth open a moment before snapping shut. "Syd," she said, a whole argument in her use of my name.

"I know," I said. "He's nuts. Cracked down the middle. Ready for the crazy train on a one way ticket to Loopyville. But, Mom, he's necessary." I hated using the very wording Fate did, but had to convince her. "His destiny is as tied to this as mine. Let me do what I've been created to do." Shudder. "What you raised me to do."

She still hesitated, I could feel it in her energy. Damn it, the last thing I needed was for her and the rest of the witches to stumble roughshod over what was supposed to be a very exclusive engagement.

"Miriam Hayle," Max said, his power filling the basement, though this time the house didn't shake, thank the elements. "Your daughter's fate was decided long before her birth. As was yours. You must follow your destiny or risk losing everything."

Mabel hummed softly in agreement, counterpoint to his words. And not just her, either. I could hear them then, the drach, speaking through her, their song heavy and ancient, but with a hint of hope.

Mom finally nodded, swallowing hard, her power backing down. I hugged her again, swiftly.

Thank you, I sent. *It's going to be okay.*

I believe it, Mom sent back, fierce and full of power. *You be safe. Always.*

I let her go. Focused on another mind, one I really barely knew.

And called Demetrius Strong.

He came as though he'd been waiting for my touch, a pool of blackness appearing before me. Demetrius's slim form danced through the empty gap, the slurping sound of it sealing behind him making me feel a little queasy. But he smiled a sunny day at me, blue eyes bright, eager as he came forward and grasped my hand, smooth cheeks as soft as any cherub, white hair curling around his face.

"Is it time, Syd?" He twitched, sorcery butting up against mine, vibrating with his excitement. "The pretty girl with the white eyes said it would be soon."

Pretty girl? Ah. Fate. Nice of her to talk to the crazy dude before me.

Grumble mumble.

Demetrius's eagerness reminded me of a puppy, kicked one too many times, but ready to trust just in case love was coming after all. Impulse drove me to hug him and, with a soft sigh of happiness, he hugged me back.

"It's time," I said, voice thick. "But I have some things to do before we go."

He pulled away, clapping his hands, feet shuffling a joyful dance as he spun in a circle.

"Okies," he said. "Ready when you are, Freddy."

I left them there, turned to the stairs, began to ascend.

"Where are you going now?" Ameline's impatience came through crystal clear.

Ignoring her felt so freaking good I was grinning by the time I reached the kitchen.

Morning had come while I was out there, wandering the planes in search of answers. Shenka sat, knees bouncing, at the table, Sassafras perched next to her. She didn't move as I smiled at them both and turned down the hall, heading for the back yard. I felt them follow, welcomed their presence as I reached hall.

Found Liam sitting at the bottom of the stairs to the second floor, waiting for me.

I took his hand, led him with me out the back door and into the soft grass and the early morning.

Dew soaked my shoes, the hem of my beat-up jeans. I felt the Wild Hunt beneath me stir, stretch in their slumber, settle again as Shaylee soothed them with a song.

I wasn't here for the Wild, though they were as much a part of me and my magic now as anyone or anything.

But no, I was here for a far different purpose. Opening my magic wide, all of my egos adding their own, my maji power pushing farther than I'd ever reached before, I called to the family.

And felt them come to me.

Mind after mind linked with me, the coven first, woken in the bright new day, their love pouring through the connection, washing over me with so much comfort I felt tears break the rims of my eyes and trickle down my cheeks. Sassafras, Shenka, Liam, Mom, the Lawrence twins... all of them, over a hundred souls, from the youngest babe to the oldest of us, gave me everything they had as I returned it.

Only one remained outside, but I would see her before I left. Had to.

Just in case my loss was her.

Onward we pushed, drawing power through the veil to Demonicon, reaching for Meira, Dad, Henemordonin, Ram. The demons answered with a roar of strength, feeding me with their power, their anger, their pride.

The Sidhe realm welcomed Shaylee, Odhran and Niamh, Unseelie and Seelie alike, even Aoilainn's magic reaching for me in the end.

The sleeping vampires woke, not to rise, but to the pressure of my presence, their consciousness aware as they embraced me with the cold glow of their power. Sunny, Uncle Frank, the Wilhelms and Sthols, though I could feel the failing of Pannera and knew her time was short. And, in a rush of magic so familiar, Sebastian, in joy.

In love.

The weres were next, Oleksander and his people howling their encouragement, Charlotte's magic giving me courage.

I never meant to go this far, only wanting to share with the ones I loved. But my reach took on its own life. I felt Max beside me, and, as though he understood this new need, his vast power added to mine and increased my reach until I had them all—the Steam Union, Piers and his mother Eva, Clover and father Felix, every one of them linked to me. Bigger, wider, more vast our touch, until we embraced all witches, all magical races. I felt Pender and his Enforcers, Femke and her people, even Quaid on the other side of the veil, in the empty plane, alive as Fate showed him to me. Safe.

And then, at last, Owen. Apollo. Trill.

The time is now, I sent to them as Max's magic hummed around me. *Be ready, be together. And know I will do everything in my power to protect you.*

Embraces, hope, and they left me, the ones I loved leaving last, until I was alone on the grass with Max holding my hand.

I turned to him, hugged him. "Thank you."

He cupped my face in his big hands. "I expected greatness," he said, "of the Light One. But you, Sydlynn, exceed all my expectations."

Choke.

One last task. The house beckoned. Her door. I

entered without knocking, found her sitting in her place, sunbeam shining over her wispy white hair, washing out her faded blue eyes. Gram's jaw was set, angry, her bare feet tapping an odd beat against the carpet.

"I'll see you," I said, amazed at how casual my voice sounded. At how light my soul felt. I really was ready, after all.

She didn't answer.

I didn't expect her to.

But as I turned to go, I heard her move, felt her hand on my arm, jerking me around.

Lost my breath as she hugged me with her whole body.

"Love you," she whispered.

"Love you, too," I said.

Gram leaned back, wiped her nose with the heel of her hand, eyes bright with tears.

"You'd damned well better come back," she snapped, "or I'm coming after you."

Maybe laughing wasn't appropriate. But I couldn't help myself.

I kissed her softly on the cheek. "I'll see you," I repeated. "And I'll have a gift for you when I'm done."

Her power. Because the moment this was over, Ameline was a dead dark maji.

Gram didn't say anything, just stood there, hands pressed to her heart, as I turned to meet my destiny.

CHAPTER TWENTY FOUR

I paused at the bottom of the stairs, caught Liam's hand where he stood, face a mask of emptiness, though I could feel his misery. He bent over me as I slid my hands into his hair, kissed him with all the passion I could muster. Felt the heat inside me, deep and thrumming, wake in answer to spread from my belly down my legs, anchoring me to the earth.

To him.

When I finally let him go, Liam pressed his lips to my forehead.

I love you so much, he sent. *And I'll be waiting when you get home.*

No doubt.

I hugged him hard, let him feel exactly what my heart thought of him. Showed him the oak tree he was to me, felt his power flare in answer.

"I'll be home for dinner," I said, turning to smile at Shenka who blinked back tears even as she smiled in return.

"We'll be here," she said. Grasped my hand a moment. Let me go.

I bent and lifted Sassafras into my arms, stroked his soft fur as his ears lay sideways, whiskers drooping, tail hanging low.

But his power hugged me all the same, the taste of it full of demon and witch alike.

No words. None were needed.

Mom took him in her arms as I handed him over. Rubbed my palms on the thighs of my jeans. Wondered in a brief, weird moment if I should go upstairs and change into a dress or something.

Silly. Get on with it then.

Right.

There was so much hate in Ameline's eyes when I met her gaze, I had to smile. "Too bad you don't have anyone to see you off," I said.

Nailed it.

She snarled and turned her back, shoulders rigid and, for a second, I actually felt sorry for her.

Naw.

Max held out his hand to me and I went to his side, amazed the butterflies I expected to make an appearance had yet to show up. Calm like I'd never known settled around me as he smiled down on me.

"Are you ready, Syd?"

Mom's question on my wedding day. Dad's.

But this day, this one was much bigger, wasn't it?

So was I?

"Let's do it." I reached for Demetrius, felt his eager quiver through our touch, turned to smile at my family.

And fell back through the veil as Max took over.

No fear, though I was falling, even then. And none when the veil opened again behind me, the endless sky above, the emptiness of the plane below, my body rushing down toward the ground.

Caught by the broad, warm back of the drach.

This time my maji power kept us safe, all of my egos flowing together, sorcery blossoming outward to mesh with all of my magicks. The world around me was suddenly brighter, cleaner, the air not quite so gray.

Full of promise. Waiting.

For me and this moment.

Demetrius laughed and clapped his hands from his perch beside me, crouching fearlessly on Max's broad shoulder. I giggled, my heart weightless, though, as I looked down, I saw them.

The army of the Brotherhood, ranks of black-robed enemy watching our approach.

They didn't attack, to my surprise, not even when Max back-winged softly to the ground, settling his forelimbs on the dead earth. A quick glance to my left showed Mabel only a moment behind, Ameline barely waiting for the drach to settle before slipping from her shoulder in a rush of maji power.

Demetrius and I dismounted together. I spun, shields protecting me from the push of air as the huge drach king rose into the air again, Mabel joining him.

Leaving us alone to face the Brotherhood.

I needn't have worried. He had just reached altitude when the sky overhead cracked in half, a giant chasm in the veil opening wide.

And the drach came pouring through.

The vision I'd seen, the one Fate showed me, had come true as what looked like an entire race of dragons hovered in square formations over our heads, waiting.

I took Demetrius's hand as he beamed at me.

"Skippidy do dah," he said. "We're off to kill the sorcerer."

I'd take that yellow brick road.

A tense wall hovered between the forward ranks of the Brotherhood and the three of us. Ameline kept a few feet distance, but stayed close enough I felt her dark maji power against mine even held tightly in check. Worry about her role in this, what Fate said to her, tried to worm its way into my calm. After all, hers was the side of chaos, the bad ending. Was she working to make it come true or did Ameline have other goals?

I just couldn't see her letting everything fall apart. She craved power over the Universe too damned much. And that fact alone eased my fear and sent it scuttling.

Fate had plans for her, I had no doubt. But the success of the Brotherhood couldn't have been on Ameline's agenda. I'd worry about what she was really up to when this thing with Belaisle was over.

Oh, wait. She'd be dead. Right. Problem solved.

I stopped about twenty feet from the first line of sorcerers, grinned when one of them looked up with a flash of fear.

"Impressive, aren't they?" I tilted my head, waving at the drach. "And they breathe fire. Did you know that?"

The line wavered. Fear pulsated so hard I felt it, not just saw it, through the sorcery part of my maji power, no longer alone but tied together with all of my magicks.

"So nice of you all to line up like this," I said. "So the drach don't have to hunt down their dinner." I grinned, letting my demon show. "Chomp chomp."

I almost had them, knew their fear traveled back through their connection to their fellows, felt it flow like a river through their ranks.

Liander Belaisle had to go and spoil my fun, didn't he?

The line of sorcerers parted in a rush as he stomped his way through them, red faced, vibrating with fury.

"Nice army," he snarled.

194

"Checkmate, asshole," I said.

In a rushed exodus, black holes appeared, the sorcerer's lines falling into them as they ran.

Cowards.

When they were done, only a handful remained, the empty plane now truly gaping and endless. But I didn't feel small, not in the least. In fact, my soul radiated, growing by the moment as my maji power spread beneath me, touching the heart of the plane.

Feeling the promise of life beneath its surface as the stronghold's power greeted me.

It was difficult to drag myself away from that hopeful feeling, to focus on the job at hand. My gaze drifted over Belaisle's shoulder to those who remained with him. Recognized faces easily.

Rupe, hulking over Mia, though, I had no doubt, not to protect but to control her. His fear felt as strong as the sorcerers who fled and I welcomed it.

The former Dumont leader alternated between shivering in her own terror and flares of fury. I moved on from her, my old concern for her well-being burned away. Her fate was her own. She'd chosen, as I'd chosen.

Destiny sucked sometimes.

"You'll get yours now!" Mia's high-pitched shriek ended in a choking sob as she pointed at me, Ameline. "You two high and mighty bitches. We'll see what's left of you when this is over."

Disgust flashed over Belaisle's face as his eyes flickered to the side. But he ignored her, expression solidifying into a smirk as his gaze settled on Demetrius.

"Brought the big guns with you, I see." He laughed even as the damaged sorcerer beside me wiggled and wriggled his continuing happiness. "What's he for? Mascot?"

Rupe laughed, too, an edge to it, Mia tittering a hysterical giggle. The only person who didn't respond on Belaisle's side glared at me with hate in her blue eyes. Alison appeared so pale, ghostly, but the taint gave her solidity at last. She might have been real and tangible again, but she wasn't the girl I knew, the bestie I'd lost to a car accident. This evil couldn't be allowed to continue.

I'd deal with her after Belaisle was a glob of bloody smear on the ground.

Belaisle's power snapped at me, tried to push me back, but my maji magic was more than a match.

I shrugged as he snarled his frustration. "I guess this will play out the way it's meant to," I said. "No cheating."

Belaisle shrugged, still cocky as he tilted his head, stroking his goatee as though things were going exactly according to plan. "We'll see," he said.

Demetrius moved, so quickly he almost pulled my arm out of its socket as he jerked me forward. Stopped and placed me exactly, giggling as he bent to move my feet just so. His hand slipped into his pocket, pulled out a sparkling blue crystal. I almost kicked myself, accepting it from him as the tiny soul inside woke and whispered its love for me.

How had I forgotten to take it?

Didn't matter. Even broken, Demetrius thought of everything.

He left me there, went for Ameline. She snarled at him but did as he said, standing across from me, south to my north, her own crystal in her hand. Belaisle came forward without urging, taking west, a flash of stone appearing out of his pocket. When Demetrius was finally satisfied, he stuck out his tongue at the dark sorcerer before stomping his foot.

Belaisle roared in anger, hopping on his undamaged one, but Demetrius was already spinning away, laughing.

Infectious, his attitude. I couldn't help but grin.

The small sorcerer turned at last, feet planted in place, east. Stopped and fell still, smiling yet, but silent. Watchful.

I had to force myself to breathe then, as time itself seemed to draw in air.

And stop.

Waiting.

This was it. The moment.

And I was ready.

chapter twenty five

Tick.

Tick.

No tock.

Nothing happened.

Um. Hmmm. Wasn't something supposed to?

I shifted my weight from one foot to the other, tension building inside me at last. Not from fear or anxiety. Just from the waiting.

Above all else, I hated waiting.

Hated.

Demetrius continued to smile, body at ease, so I took my cue from him, tried to relax.

Whatever was coming, I had to believe it could only happen in exactly the right way.

Still.

Sigh. Couldn't we just freaking get on with it already?

I mean, seriously. Hadn't Fate invested a ton of time and effort into this thing? Only to make us stand there and stare at each other like a bunch of idiots with no clue what to do next?

I was pretty sure Demetrius knew. But it seemed wrong to ask.

Hang on. Something was missing. The image I'd seen, the one Fate showed me at her fountain, included Quaid. Trill. Owen and Apollo. Where were they?

Belaisle's cockiness fell away as time continued to hold still and wait. Worry flickered, followed by anger. Fear. Tension. Nice to know he was freaked while my soul continued to sit, in peace, though the waiting was really going to kill me.

"This is ridiculous," Ameline snapped.

As if her words began something, the air beside her crackled, parted and Trinol stepped through. She glanced up at him. Was that relief on her face?

I didn't have time to find out, not when Iepa appeared next to me, set one hand on my shoulder.

"Just kill them, Liander!" Mia's voice pierced our circle, though none of us paid attention.

Not when the moment was so close.

I was so tied to the circle I stood in, the held breath of time, I almost missed the press of emptiness above me, only looking up when Belaisle laughed.

My heart contracted, peace shattered, as the air over

the drach parted in pools of black and the Brotherhood fell through.

"Finally," he said, meeting my eyes with a smile. "This will be over before you know it."

I could feel the power drain, the loss of magic as the drach tried to fight. Fell beneath the combined pressure of the Brotherhood's power and the siphoning pull of the stronghold.

"No," I whispered, tears burning my eyes as the mighty first race began to spiral to the ground, weakened, drained, all of their magic leaving them, through the sorcerers, filling the gaping, endless hole of the giant stronghold.

This wasn't what I'd seen. The vision I witnessed had the drach fighting the Brotherhood on the ground, fire and magic making a mess of Belaisle's ranks. And the four I sought.

Where were they?

I spun on Iepa, trembling, reaching for her, but she shook her head, wouldn't look up even as the first drach hit the ground, the impact so hard my knees buckled.

"Thank you for bringing your little dragon friends," Belaisle said. "You really must learn I will always be ahead of your thinking, dear Sydlynn. And that you played, as usual, right into my hands."

Bastard. I spun with a snarl, maji power keeping me stable as more of the dragon folk hit the ground, the empty plane around us suddenly full of fallen bodies, hovering Brotherhood standing over them in groups of three and four, clinging to the weakening drach like leeches.

But when I tried to stop it, my power lashing outward, I hit a wall.

The circle we stood in trapped my magic and refused to let me save them.

I knew it was Max the moment he crashed, shoulder first, not ten feet from me, diamond eyes locked on mine. The sky was now empty, gray, dismal while my heart broke for the mighty drach.

"Why are you letting this happen?" I wanted to hit Iepa, fists balled at my sides.

"I'm not," she said in a soft wail. "This is Fate, Syd."

"Excellent," Belaisle said, rubbing his hands together. Gestured to Rupe.

My old friend, once the Goth known as Blood, now Belaisle's creature, smirked and turned, opening a black hole even as the stronghold reached for me.

Your friends are alive, he sent, deep voice crushing stone. *But something isn't right.*

Quaid tumbled out, Trill on top of him, the Zornov brothers collapsing next to them just as the gap closed with a snap.

"Ah, our last guests have arrived." Belaisle bowed to me. "I had planned to take them myself, but you delivered them to me with perfect timing." He ignored my fury, his voice expanding, echoing as he spoke to his people. "Now, my brothers and sisters. Use their power to do as instructed. The planes are ours."

No. No! I fought against the wall of Fate as Trill cried out, head lifting, iridescence filling her gaze. Owen surged to his feet, blackness flowing around him while Apollo stood, jerking Trill up to join them. The three held hands, their connection solidifying just as the drach cried out as a people.

Giant gashes filled the sky. Demonicon's amber sky shone through one, the green scape of the Sidhe another. And the blue of my home, the slice cut open over Wilding Springs.

I felt them cry out, call to me, the wall allowing me to feel them even as it prevented me from saving the very ones I'd only just embraced. Demon, Sidhe, vampire, witch, sorcerer, all falling, their power flowing through the helpless drach, with the Zornovs as the focus, into the Brotherhood.

And to the stronghold's bottomless gullet of need.

Please, stop the drain! I reached for the stronghold's mind, but found only blank greed. He had to be in there somewhere, but the force-feeding of so much power must have shut off his consciousness, leaving only the siphoning monster behind.

I wept as I battered myself against Fate, begged, fell

to my knees as I felt Shenka, Sassafras, Mom, Meira, all of them, my beloved ones, their power flowing in a ruptured hemorrhage I could do nothing to quell.

Belaisle's chuckling made it worse. "Little did you know," he said, "that by bringing me the drach, the masters of the veil, paired with the darling Zornov trio, you left your people at my mercy." He snorted. "All to follow some silly prophecy. You're more a fool than I ever thought, Sydlynn Hayle." Belaisle's power slapped me, jerking me out of my despair. "Thank you for giving me everything."

I staggered to my feet, heart aching, swiping the tears of agony from my face as power continued to gush out of the gashes between planes. But it was slowing, less and less flowing, coming to an end.

I saw it, watched its path, felt the understanding like a blow to my chest as the peak of the tower absorbed the magic, down into the heart of the stronghold. Belaisle saw me looking, of course he did, the bastard. Had clearly been waiting for me to notice just exactly what the siphon's focus was.

"This place was made to hold power," Belaisle said, an evil teacher with a gleeful tone.

"But not by you," Demetrius said.

Still smiling his cherub smile.

He'd finally lost his mind completely.

Belaisle's frown told me it was true. "We understood

it," he said. "Used it for our purpose. And when the maji chased us from this place, we never forgot." Belaisle's eyes locked on mine. "It fed on the Enforcers, slowly gathering power. But I knew it needed the souls of maji to make our plan work." He grinned, teeth flashing, no humor in it. "Opening the power to the place, starting the transfer required the three children you gifted me. But granting me control over everything…" Belaisle threw his arms wide. "That required two very specific maji."

Oh. My. Swear—

"Did you think you were the only two with Fate on your side?" Belaisle jammed his hands into the pockets of his expensive suit, beaming much as Demetrius beamed at me, though without the small sorcerer's dreamy calm. "We have our own course to follow. And we've won, haven't we?" He tsked. "A shame you didn't put up much of a fight. I expected so much more from the great Light and Dark."

I stared up at the tower, knowing then this was my fault, Ameline's. Our power allowed this to happen.

The planes were going to fall and there was nothing I could do about it.

No, no, this couldn't be right! Fate showed me, led me to believe I had a chance...

She was wrong.

It was over.

Demetrius leaned toward me, took my hand, his

sorcery bumping my power as his eyes sparkled with joy.

You fight, his mind slipped into mine, *when you should just embrace your destiny.*

Was he mad? Yes. Mad, lost, broken.

And yet.

It was so hard to stop fighting, to force myself to relax. Fate told me I needed to trust him, but it was difficult, painful, to ease, search for the peace I'd come here with. Leap of faith to the nth degree making my stomach cramp. Had to close my eyes, draw deep breaths, while Demetrius's steady power soothed me and the crystal in my hand hummed with happiness.

There, I felt it finally, the wall of Fate coming down. But when I snatched at my power, tried to fight again, the barrier slammed back into place. Was that the key, really? I was going to fail, my fear flailing around.

More breathing, seeming endless agony, wanting to hurry when only slow and steady gave me what I needed.

Peace. Calm. And the pull of the stronghold.

It wanted me, my magic. Began to drain me the moment Fate's wall finally collapsed. I heard Ameline gasp as I released a deep and wrenching sob, clinging to Demetrius's hand.

This was my task? To give in to the pull, to lower the wall and allow us to be drained?

Was Fate freaking loony?

I can't, I sent, frantic need beating at the edges of my

forced calm. *I won't be able to fight if I let go.*

And yet, he sent, *this is your fate, Syd.*

It couldn't be. Fate wouldn't want me to fail, to let the planes die.

I opened my eyes, saw the tears standing in his big blues, the trembling smile on his lips as Ameline's power recoiled, lost the fight.

"What are you doing!" She screamed at me, struggled to keep her magic, Belaisle laughing, laughing.

What will this solve? I clung to the damaged sorcerer, desperate for any reason to believe. *It will only give Belaisle his victory, more power. How is this right?*

You must, he sent, soft, lovely in the midst of ugly hurt. *Trust me.*

So. Hard.

With a last embrace to my egos, their own resolve slipping as we clung to each other a long, lonely moment, I gave up.

Gave in.

And let the stronghold take everything I had.

Ameline shrieked at the sky as her power flowed out of her, following mine. She glared at me, hate twisting her face, spit flying from her lips as she screamed incoherently.

I didn't care. Not when I felt them leave me, one by one, my souls, my sisters. Nothing else mattered.

Ameline spun on Trinol. "This wasn't the

agreement!" She hit him hard in the chest with both fists, rocking him back with a shocked expression on his face. "I will not die for this foolishness!"

I had enough magic left to feel the planes crumbling on the other side of the gashes, their edges cracking. Demonicon hovered on the edge of breaking, though I felt the Node hanging on far better than I expected it to.

Not much longer now and it would all be over.

I almost welcomed it as I sagged to my knees, weak, almost empty.

Fate was wrong. And I would rather not see how it ended, thanks.

I looked up, met Ameline's eyes as she fell, too. She clawed at the ground, pulled herself toward me, hand finally landing on mine.

Severing the last connection we both had to our power the moment we touched.

chapter twenty six

So this was what it felt like to be normal. I'd thought I known, back when I lost my demon, my witch magic still trapped behind the spell of protection Gram placed over her own power, holding me down and dull.

And yet, I had no idea even then I had magic, that Gram's watched over me, lived inside me, gave me more feeling and awareness than I believed.

Until I sat there, my enemy panting with her head in my lap, empty and ordinary.

Mortal.

Ameline forced herself up, bared her teeth at me in a fierce snarl, tears on her cheeks, blue eyes full of rage and hate and horrible terror.

"You bitch," she said, voice softer than air despite her expression. "You've destroyed us all."

I looked up at the gashes in the veils, saw the flow of

power had stopped. Demonicon was still there, not destroyed, the other planes looking dull. Or maybe that was just my normal eyesight.

"Wouldn't do to destroy the very places we wish to rule." Belaisle stood over us, smiling his smirk of victory as he tilted his head and nudged Ameline with the toe of one polished shoe. "The power we've taken will do. For now."

Wind whipped a sudden gale, icy. So cold I hugged myself, thin t-shirt doing nothing to keep me warm. The sudden feeling of temperature again made me shiver, another reminder I'd lost everything as my silent mind sought out the voices of those who shared my head.

Came up empty.

The once gray sky looked darker to me, clouds forming in a place only grayness once lived. I felt someone hit me from behind, turned, looked up to see Mia, ice blue eyes wild, hunched next to me.

She poked me again, harder this time, painfully, sure to leave a bruise. Black makeup tracked down her pale cheeks, her deep red lipstick smeared as she wiped her running nose with the back of her hand. "How does it feel," she hissed, "to be nothing?"

I didn't answer.

Because I didn't have one for her.

Mia lunged for Belaisle, hugging his leg even as Rupe rushed forward to lift her free of the disgusted sorcerer.

"Please," she begged, snot running down her face, her nails clawing at her white cheeks. "You promised you'd give me some." She reached for him with black-painted nails ragged and bloody, sobbing, shattered. "Please, you said you would."

He ignored her as Rupe tossed the scrawny Dumont witch to the ground next to the silently waiting Zornovs. Now that the transfer was done, they stood, quiet and as lost as I was, trapped in thrall to the Brotherhood. Quaid seemed free of Belaisle, but from the way his hands shook as he looked at them, his power was gone, too.

"Fool," Alison hissed at Mia, drawing my attention back, the former echo's fangs lengthening. "He only used you to get to Syd in the first place."

Mia's sobbing stopped, eyes huge and staring at the ghostly Alison.

"No," she whispered. Turned to look at me. And made me watch as the girl she was finally died behind her eyes.

My own soul crumbled at the death of hers. And I know I would have fallen into my own endless despair, if it wasn't for the sky.

For the flare of power overhead drawing my eyes up, up to the peak of the stronghold tower.

Where two swirling masses of magic came together. Giant, shining with iridescence, my maji magic. Ameline's. Whirling like two tornadoes at the peak, dancing together in harmony over the heart spike of the stronghold.

"And now," Belaisle said, "I have the power to remake the Universe as it was meant to be." He winked at me. "In my image." He drew a great breath, let it out in a gust of happiness, clapping his hands together. "Well now," he said. "Where to begin?"

Demetrius's blue eyes crawled with black before he chuckled.

"Why," he said, "with me. Naturally."

And threw a giant ball of emptiness right at the leader of the Brotherhood.

I pulled Ameline toward me, out of the line of fire and, despite our animosity, the two of us huddled together, both held in place by the battle going on in front of us.

Rupe tried to interfere, his sorcery swelling to slice at Demetrius, but instead of landing the blow, it recoiled, as though thrown back in his face. The tall, former friend of mine fell away with a cry, landing hard on his ass, his own magic engulfing and smothering him.

Even normal, I felt the Brotherhood physically sway, the gathered sorcerers still pinning the drach to the ground watching, waiting for their master to defeat Demetrius.

Didn't happen. To my amazement, though the first blow he threw was dispelled by Belaisle, Demetrius answered the now furious Brotherhood leader's counterattack with one of his own.

While Belaisle seemed to hunker down to fight, his missed attempts shaking the very plane itself as he brought his power to bear, Demetrius's movements were a dance as he battered his opponent with balls of soul-sucking blackness, leaping out of the way in time to snare the other's power and use it for his own. A small relief woke inside me as I understood no matter how much Belaisle had access to, he was still a sorcerer. A thief who could only use other's power as a source, not add it to his own.

A tiny comfort. But I'd take it.

The longer their fight went on, the more furious Belaisle became until he roared in rage, lifting one arm, a massive hammer of darkness rising above him.

Ready to crush Demetrius Strong.

The air between the dueling sorcerers shimmered before Belaisle could strike and two young maji appeared, eyes white, faces serene. Light Fate nodded to me before turning her head toward Demetrius. "Mine is damaged," she said, "but his heart is whole."

"True," her brother said, empty eyes fixed on Belaisle, "but mine has access to more power."

So Belaisle lied to me, didn't he? About having his own Fate.

The fact they stood there seemed to infuriate the Brotherhood leader. "You don't rule me!" His voice carried, echoing back from the walls of the stronghold. "I am my own Fate!"

I almost laughed, was too tired, drained. But I did inside my head, just a little.

"I will hunt you both," he snarled, madness in his eyes as his face purpled in rage, "and I will kill you after making you suffer and suffer and suffer."

Demetrius giggled, both hands over his mouth, eyes sparkling with mirth. "You're too weak," he said. "Even with all the power of the planes at your disposal. You'll never be strong enough to fight Fate, Liander. Never."

At least he sounded lucid. Maybe he could do some good after all.

Belaisle's eyes lit up as Demetrius finished, the madness in him surging as he laughed at the sky.

"Perfect," he said. And reached out with both hands toward the stronghold.

Belaisle hadn't been using all the magic he had access to.

That was about to change.

His body began to change, grow, expanding as his shoulders shot upward into the gathering storm overhead. His laughter now rumbled like the thunder, sparks falling from his fingers in flares like lightening.

"I am Fate," he boomed, looming over us, black doom painting his eyes the color of his power.

Demetrius's smile didn't waver as he bent beside me

and held out his hand.

"I need your crystal," he said with perfect clarity. "If you don't mind."

I gaped at him. Looked down at it in my hand even as Belaisle's giant foot shifted next to me, rising to crush us all like bugs.

My hand lurched forward, dropped the silent stone into Demetrius's hand. He liberated Ameline's from hers without asking. Stood swiftly, turned and bowed to the Fates who seemed unconcerned Belaisle's massive foot was about to come down on them.

Looked up with his bright blue eyes.

And grew.

Belaisle staggered as Demetrius rose to meet him, the ground-cracking vibration of his foot touching down bouncing me from the barren dirt before dropping me again. The whole plane rumbled with the pressure of Belaisle's step, though, amazingly, no one was crushed, his focus not with us anymore.

But on the beaming cherub who faced him down, two massive crystals in his hands.

"Thanks for coming by," Demetrius said. "But the party's over."

The two silent stones suddenly blazed, the blue with light, the black with fire, and drew in power in a rush so powerful the air around me boomed from the sonic shift.

chapter twenty seven

Two titans faced off above us, magic flowing from the stronghold, through Belaisle and the gathering storm and into the crystals Demetrius held in his hands.

"No!" Belaisle's denial reverberated, my ears aching from the sound.

"You were so certain you broke me," Demetrius said, voice softer, but still overwhelming as the gush of power diving for the crystals increased in speed, the wind it raised battering me, forcing me to hunch forward with my face pressed into Ameline's shoulder and hers to mine. But I still heard the sorcerer speak.

Every word.

"I did break you!" I tried to look up, caught a glimpse of Belaisle striking at Demetrius with one fist, but the former Steam Union sorcerer simply twisted to the side, the blow going wide.

"You didn't," Demetrius said in his kind and gentle voice. "I held on, Liander. Even after you killed my parents. Even after you threatened the love of my heart. Even when you crushed me and took my power." Tears rose in my eyes, my heart constricting for all of the pain he endured only to be here, now, in this place, facing the one who tried to ruin him. "And yet, I remain, don't I, Liander? And I have Fate to thank." Demetrius looked down at the smiling maji girl. "I am Steam Union," he said in a deep and resounding voice, "and I always will be."

A crack of thunder jolted me as lightning hit the ground only a heartbeat before, making my hair stand on end, the scent of crisping ozone burning my nose.

At the very same moment, I heard the drach begin to sing.

Heart surging with hope, I looked up completely, no longer willing to peek, shading my squinting eyes from debris. Trill and her brothers were in action again, channeling power back the other way. Into the drach.

The dragons surged as one to their feet, dumping the screaming Brotherhood to the ground.

Demetrius held out his hands at shoulder height, the exodus of power through Belaisle now flowing outward from the crystals and into the Zornovs far faster than it left. Better, it flew through the drach, upward into the gashes in the veil, returning in a rush to the planes from where it had been taken.

"Your arrogance was your Fate," Demetrius said as Belaisle screamed and began to shrink at last, in jerking, painful looking steps, his body contorting as one arm shriveled, one side of his face, his right hip, down, down until he was just himself again.

The wind died, slowed to a breeze as the magic went home. I looked up, tears running down my face, to see the gashes heal, closing behind the power, restoring what had been damaged until only a soft breath of air remained.

Stilled.

Went quiet.

The sudden silence was almost painful as I released Ameline, openly weeping in relief. I might have been empty, but the planes were safe. My family, the ones I loved.

It was all that mattered to me.

Trill and her brothers collapsed, Quaid immediately going to them, protecting them as his eyes flared with blue fire, power restored. He looked shocked when he caught my eyes, sadness flickering over his face.

Yes, his magic was back. But mine...

Gone. Maybe forever.

Was this my loss?

Demetrius had shrunk himself, now the diminutive, sweet-faced sorcerer I knew. But no longer did a scar mar his face, his white hair thick and lustrous, body held with pride and power. He turned to me, not a hint of madness in his eyes as he blew me a kiss.

I laughed through my tears and caught it, pressed it to my heart.

But how?

"You forgot," Demetrius said, comforting in his way, as Belaisle fell to his knees with a howl of rage. "The very power you used to draw the magicks to you lives in the crystals tied to the maji you tried to manipulate." He tossed them both in his hands, their cores now full of power again, glowing like small stars in his grip. "The moment you accessed the power of the stronghold, you left yourself—and those magicks—open to me. And the crystals."

The drach roared, still melodious, but full of joy, filling the air with the sound of their approval.

Belaisle's body crumpled further as, I could only guess, the crystals continued to siphon from him. "Brother," he croaked, reaching for Demetrius. "We could have ruled the Universe together." He gasped for a breath as his face began to age, skin wrinkling, eyes sinking into their sockets. "Don't give up all that power."

The drach rose into the air, the backwash of their wing strokes buffeting me all over again. But I didn't mind, rejoiced at their recovery as they hovered above, their power pinning the fallen and now powerless

Brotherhood to the ground.

"Power?" Demetrius's smile was angelic. "I have the greatest of all power, Liander. I have my sanity back."

Belaisle sighed as he finally collapsed and fell still. But I wasn't looking at him anymore.

My gaze followed Demetrius as he turned to me, the weeping Ameline who clutched me light a frightened child, and held out his hands.

And the glowing crystals he held.

New hope joined with the old, a spark so pure I struggled to move, to take what he offered, my mind unable to accept maybe, just maybe, we'd won after all.

And that the crystal before me held the life I thought I lost.

White power flared, a figure moving with frightening speed toward the smiling sorcerer, a hand lashing toward my crystal. I cried out in fear, longing making me more afraid than the sight of Alison, her ghostly face pinched in fury, trying to take what was mine.

Demetrius spun, gestured. And the two crystals came together in her face. A giant spark leaped from the two as they clinked together, flying from their glowing surfaces to land on Alison's chest.

She screamed as the spark burrowed inside her, clawed at herself, entire form taking on the same glow as the fire she'd absorbed, until her entire body flung outward in a flare of light.

And she was gone.

I let my hands fall, hoping she'd finally moved on to a better place, even as my secret fear all was lost burned its own hole inside me.

But Demetrius's smile was as sweet as ever as he returned his attention to us, as though nothing happened. "For you," he said. "With thanks."

Ameline snatched hers, gasped out loud as power jerked her upright. I clutched at Demetrius's hand, feeling a tingle race over my fingertips as they passed across the surface of the crystal.

And my power slammed back into me in a single blow.

Syd! My demon's fire scorched me in her eagerness to reach me.

Syd! Shaylee sang my name as Sidhe power shook me from my toes to the top of my head.

Sydlynn, my vampire sent, cold sizzle of her spirit magic filling me up again.

The family magic surged its joy, spinning in dizzy circles, making me a little queasy, while the black blossom of my sorcery opened wide, full, for the moment, not hungry.

And as they came together, their joy at being with me again, my maji power burst forth in a brilliant light of rainbow flare, puncturing the clouds over head.

And the sky opened.

I looked down from the wonder of it, drenched in the sudden downpour where I was sure no rain had ever fallen, to see the fierce happiness on Ameline's face, knew she, too, was restored.

Turned to find Belaisle, gray and withered, crawling from the circle we'd made. Took a step toward him even as Rupe, panting from his battle with his sorcery, dove for his master.

I tried to catch them, pull them back. But the wall of Fate rose and held me back. Forcing me to watch as the pair fell through a gaping black hole, the snarl on Rupe's face telling me that for him, this wasn't over.

But it was. I wiped rain from my face, laughing as my power retreated from the wall, smiling at Fate.

I have other plans for those two, she sent to me, her mind so large I finally had to retreat from my need to see just how far it went. *Now that the path ahead is clear.*

I was in as about a trusting mood as I'd ever felt, so I just nodded. Let it go. Let them go.

I had no doubt I'd get another chance to kill Liander Belaisle.

Light One, the stronghold reached for me. *My fate is now at hand. And I have you to thank. For so long I've waited for this day. I am the center of everything. And now, all life can find its way to me at last.*

The torrent of rain eased as quickly as it began and, as the clouds shivered and parted, blue sky, bright and welcoming, appeared, a full and happy sun where once none hung, shone down over the empty plane.

Mia's weeping drew my attention from the amazing change around me, her body crumpling at last into a small ball of shattered life, hope, love. I reached for her with power, felt my maji ability stretch, bigger and stronger than before, and eased her into sleep.

Demetrius came to my side, kissed my cheek. "You leave Liander and Rupe to me," he said. "They are my Fate, in case you didn't know."

I hadn't. Squeezed his hand. "You're leaving me." Why did that make me want to hug him and cry like a little girl?

"You'll see me again." He drew a deep breath, arms wide, smile just as much so, before a black portal appeared behind him. "Tell Ethpeal I'll be by to check on her soon."

And fell backward into it before it swallowed him up and snapped shut.

Gram. He'd mentioned Gram.

But Fate said... did that mean I wasn't going to lose her?

More hope. I dared believe.

I turned to Fate to ask her, only to hear the sound of the very plane around me.

Inhaling.

chapter twenty eight

My Fate's lovely face turned upward as she spread her hands. Her brother bowed to her and vanished, but not before also bowing to me.

The familiar presence of Max pressed against my back, his power deep and as vast as ever as Fate whistled a song in the expanding air. When she dropped her empty eyes to mine, she unpursed her lips to smile.

"Well done, my very dear Sydlynn," she said. Her head shifted a fraction, blank gaze over my shoulder. "Oh, my love," she said. "You're strong enough."

I felt him shiver, half-turned to look up at him, only to swing back as she vanished.

And gasped in awe as the ground beneath my feet erupted into green and blue and red and pink. All shades of deepest emerald, jewel toned flowers flourishing in full bloom on the suddenly thick, lush carpet of grass, trees leaping, full-formed from the earth, reaching for the blue, blue sky.

Within the time it took me to catch my breath, the empty plane was empty no longer, the sound of bird song and the chitter of small animals the most beautiful music I'd ever heard.

"It waited for this moment," Max said. "For you to free its soul."

His. The soul of the plane. I touched him again, felt the power of the stronghold embrace me, feeding magic until I pulled free, already stretched further and with more power than I knew what to do with.

But when I turned to look for Ameline, to share this wonder with her despite our differences, she was already gone.

But before I could panic, freak out over her escape as I came back to myself, shaking off the awe of what I just went through and returned to good old cynicism—my favorite—Iepa just shrugged, her own tears on her face.

"It's over," she said. "You can do what you want now."

No sweeter words had ever been spoken.

I could finally kill Ameline and take Gram's power back. Ahbi's. And kill that bitch once and for all.

Hesitated, feeling doubt clench tight around my chest, not about Ameline, but about what happened here.

And why.

Iepa must have known what I was going to ask. She came to me, took my hand, squeezed it in hers. "It was about choice, Sydlynn," she said. "Isn't it always? Didn't Fate tell you so?"

I nodded, mind churning around what she said as she went on.

"Without your choice to trust Demetrius, to trust Fate, having faith no matter the loss to yourself, to those you loved, you would have fallen. A fight would have led to the battle I showed you when we first met." I shivered at the memory, all those witches, demons, every one, dead at the hands of the Brotherhood. "Ameline was never the center of this and, had Fate not needed her power to complete the circle and lure Belaisle, only you would have been necessary."

To make a choice. Imagine that.

"I almost didn't." The words escaped me in a whisper, fearful as I realized what my stubbornness could have meant.

"But," Iepa said, smoothing my hair back from my face, "you did. As Fate knew you would. With your faith to heal him, Demetrius's choice to give up the power he took from Belaisle, to return it from where it was stolen, completed his restoration." She sighed softly, dropped her hands. "Dark Fate never believed you would sacrifice so much, that Demetrius would give up what Belaisle craved. And, because of that, Light won."

Okay then.

"And Ameline?" What was her fate? "If she wasn't here to fulfill a purpose?"

Iepa hesitated. "Her fate has yet to appear," she said. "Her choice."

She'd better hurry up. Time was ticking on her final clock, you betcha.

Mia's sobbing stilled as she looked up suddenly, faint smile on her face.

"Hello?" She staggered to her feet, looking around with an air of innocence I would have more closely paired to a child. "How pretty." She bent, plucked a flower, smelled it. Giggled.

Iepa's sad smile lifted to Max. He gestured and two of his drach shifted to human shape, coming to take Mia by the hand and lead her away. She turned to me as they left, blue eyes blinking as she smiled at me.

"Her mind is gone," Iepa said. "And with it, her pain and the memories of what she became in the end." She nodded once, as though there were no other choice to be made. "You are very generous, Sydlynn."

Considering I didn't know what I was doing when I put Mia into sleep, Iepa was being kind of generous herself. Still, I was glad the broken witch found some of her own peace.

"My people will guard over her," Max said. "Until such time your Enforcers return to take over."

226

I turned to him, hugged him. "Thank you," I said. "I'm so sorry your people had to suffer for this to work out."

He held me gently against him, face so sad I wished there was more I could do or say to make him feel better.

"I have to find Ameline." I stepped away from him. Max nodded, head hanging, shoulders slumped just a little.

"As do I," he said. "I will come with you." He finally looked up again, diamond eyes moist. "As is my task."

Why did that make him so unhappy? Maybe his people didn't kill, didn't believe in it or something?

What was I missing?

Didn't matter. I'd sort it all out later. For now, I had one job and one job only.

Find that bitch and make sure her death was slow and painful.

I turned to go, spotted my friends, and totally forgot Ameline. Rushed to Trill who sat up, shaking her head, looking around with huge, brown eyes.

"What happened?" She helped Owen sit up as Quaid assisted Apollo. "Syd, is it over?" She smiled in childish wonder at the beauty around her, running her hands through the grass. "We won?"

I hugged her, laughed. "You were a big help," I said.

Owen grabbed me next, brilliant blue eyes narrowed under a frown as he let me go. "Syd, are you being sarcastic?"

"I'm not," I said. "For once." Nudged Apollo's sneaker. "Nice job, you three."

Met Quaid's eyes.

I'm sorry. Guilt almost choked me, it showed up so fast.

For what? His Enforcer magic warmed me up. *Saving everyone?*

I left you behind. How could I explain to him how hard it was to do that?

You did what you had to do, he sent. *And we're fine.*

He was, too. Looked fabulous, dark waves all tousled and chocolate eyes full of yumminess.

Married.

Happily.

Yup.

Time to go. I helped Trill to her feet, waited while Owen dusted off the seat of his jeans, Apollo winking at me.

"A chick with power and a hot bod," he said. "What's not to love?"

I laughed. Didn't smack him.

Went home instead.

chapter twenty nine

I passed us through the veil, felt Mom reach for me the moment my feet touched down in the back yard. Liam wasn't home, I could tell immediately, felt his presence pulse at the wards to the Sidhe cavern. He was safe, at least.

Our reunion would have to wait.

Syd. Mom's power hugged me, desperate before releasing me again. *What happened?*

Quaid and the Zornovs gave me space, Max an immobile statue watching me as I turned away, eyes locked on the park beyond our back yard, mind focused on my mother.

Long, crazy, you'll never believe it story, I sent. *Is everyone okay?*

Yes, of course, she sent. *Frightened and shaken, but whatever happened was over so fast we didn't have time to react between feeling like our magic was gone to everything snapping back into place again.*

Whoa. What felt like forever to me had been an instant to them. Probably a good thing. Though knowing time literally held its breath while I made up my damned mind gave me the willies.

Short version, I sent, *we won. The stronghold is empty, though there's an army of drach there standing guard over the fallen Brotherhood, so you might want to move your Enforcer's butts before Max's people take over for good.*

Not that I was really worried, but it felt good to joke about something.

Anything.

Oh, I sent as an afterthought while her mind branched off from mine, probably to talk to Pender. *Mia Dumont is in their custody too. Mom.* I hesitated. *She doesn't remember anything.*

Mom's sadness told me what I needed to know. *You realize it won't matter*, she sent. *The law is the law. And the Councils will be looking for someone to punish.*

I know. I let it go, handed it over to Mom to let her deal with.

I had other things to think about.

I'm going after Ameline. I know Mom must have felt the satisfaction in my magic, because it ripped through me in a powerful flash of absolute horrendous joy.

Save me a piece, Mom said, equally vicious.

We'll see.

I looked up at Max, felt his sorrow hovering around him, pushed my empathy for his feelings aside. "I need help," I said. "Can you track her through the veil?"

He nodded, took my hand again. "Like this," he said. And left Quaid and the Zornovs behind, carrying me into the place between planes.

I saw her path immediately, cold and tingling, old from the way it sparked in tiny pinpoints.

She was here once, Max sent.

The day she attacked Gram. Perfect. Except.

She's been a lot of places since here, I sent. *I'd rather not retrace every single time she's been in the veil.*

Agreed, he sent. *Then call to her power and find its most recent trail.*

Interesting. I opened my maji power, connected with Ameline's, remembering the feeling of her, of Ahbi and Gram, of the Sidhe soul she carried, of the darkness of Belaisle's sorcery and the taint of the vampire's thrall.

Like a rubber band snapping into place, I traveled in a straight shot to connect with her, the tingling buzz of my first discovery burning with fresh power.

Excitement heated my heart. *She was here recently*, I sent, eagerness set on explode.

She was, Max sent. *But a day ago.*

Damn it. I focused tighter, now that I knew how her path felt. Connected again with an even more powerful trail.

But this time it was easier for me to decipher the frame of reference, hours passed, distance. *She was here last*, I sent. *But before the battle. Where the hell were we?* A soft touch to the edge of the veil told me. Core.

The home of the dark maji.

No wonder her trail thrummed and hummed and sizzled along my power. Because it wasn't just hers I sensed, but mine, too. Max and Mabel's. Now that I knew where I was, what I was feeling, I could separate our trails from hers.

Again, Max sent. *But only Ameline.*

Only Ameline.

I knew I had the hang of it now, felt Max's support, his approval as I maneuvered the veil, able to feel the separation between planes. Feeling the veil keeping my home from Demonicon was only a small section, the veil itself going on and on, a labyrinth of walls and doorways, gates and sealed worlds, all bound together by the slippery, rubber membrane around me.

I pulled to a halt finally, near home, frustrated and irritated. The only path of Ameline's I could find was wrong, all wrong. Thinking I was smart, I returned to the stronghold plane in what felt like—and I now knew was—the center of everything, and went looking. But her energy there was missing demon power and Sidhe, weaker than I'd felt her in a long time.

Had to be an old trail.

Craptastic. I felt Max beside me, hovering, waiting in silence. *I lost her. Which meant she had to be back at the stronghold, hadn't entered the veil at all. Do we go back?*

She's not at the stronghold, he sent with so much conviction I instantly believed him.

Fine, not there. Then I would check in with every single race I knew, even if I had to tear the planes apart one at a time to find her.

First stop was a no brainer and I was glad I made it the moment I stepped out of the veil and into the Sidhe Gate cavern. Liam came running at once, swinging me into his arms, face pressed to my neck as he whispered his love to me over and over again. I kissed him, legs twined around his waist, laughing and breathless over his mouth as he leaned away and smiled.

"I knew it," he said. "My hero."

I laughed, head back, loud and ringing. "Smartass husband," I said. Kissed him a little more thoroughly while the heat of our connection crawled down my stomach and legs.

"I mean it," he said. "You're the most amazing and best thing that has ever happened to me and I can't believe you're my wife."

Sniffle. "Even though I'm a trouble magnet?" I giggled. "And almost get everyone—including myself—killed on a regular basis?"

"Because of that," he said. "I love trouble. You didn't know?"

Galleytrot cleared his throat, waggling his doggy brows suggestively as his big tongue lolled out the side of his mouth. But his tail was wagging and, when Liam set me down, the big dog rumbled a happy greeting as I hugged him hard.

"Nice to see you safe and sound," he said.

"You, too." I straightened, sighed. "I'm only here for a minute. I'll tell you everything later. But right now, I'm hunting Ameline."

Liam's frown told me immediately he wasn't happy about this turn of events. "Where is she?"

"Silly," I said, "if I knew that, she's be dead already."

Galleytrot growled. "Is she on this plane?"

I hesitated. "Don't know," I said. "Something's wonky." I turned to Max who watched me with his sad diamond eyes. "Could she have masked her trail somehow, knowing I'd be after her?"

"Possible," he said. "Perhaps we'll have more luck if we search for that trail on the actual planes themselves."

Wow. "I can do that?"

He smiled, though it didn't take away his odd grief. "You can. And you already know how."

Wicked cool.

I kissed Liam one more time, went to Max, took his big hand. Turned and blew my husband one last smooch while he closed the gap between himself and the giant hound, hand on Galleytrot's head as we stepped back into the veil.

And out again on the other side of the Sidhe wards.

Now, Max's voice sent. *Look.*

I did as he'd taught me in the veil itself, seeking out Ameline. Felt her touch with the vampires, though I knew it was probably an old trail.

Stepped through the veil to Castle Wilhelm anyway.

Chapter Thirty

I smiled as Chambrelle Strait greeted me with a smile and a bow just as the sun set.

"Perfect timing," she said, red hair twisted into a no-nonsense knot, pale green eyes sparkling. "Her Majesty will be rising soon."

"Her Majesty has already risen." I turned to the sound of Sunny's voice, ran to hug her, Uncle Frank, as the pair of them, bodies still cold from sleep, squeezed me between them.

Good thing my temperature sensation was turned off again. Nothing worse than being the center of a vampire sandwich before they had breakfast.

They pelted me with questions, most of which I deflected as I had with Mom.

"Later," I said. "I'm still looking for Ameline."

Sunny promised to have her network search while I

offered one last round of hugs and headed out again. This time to Ukraine, the palace.

Charlotte's arms were so strong, so tight around me, if I hadn't been invincible I was sure she'd have cracked more than a few ribs. When she let me go, she coughed softly, head down, hiding the tears I knew she struggled to contain.

"Ameline," I said. "Everything comes after I find her."

Another promise, this one from Oleksander as he sent me off, calling to his people to find the witch and pin her down so I could kill her slowly.

I loved the werewolves.

You do realize they won't catch her, Max sent.

I do, I sent back as we skimmed through the veil on the way to the Sidhe realm. *But maybe I can keep her running and hiding, off balance a little. Besides, you have no idea how great it is just to touch base with everyone. Considering what happened.*

What could have happened.

Max didn't respond, his odd sorrow rising again and I wondered if his sadness was for himself. Had his people lost more than I thought in this fight? Whatever I could do to help him, I swore to myself, I would. After all he'd done to protect and guide me, it was the least I could do.

Ameline first. Everything else after.

Aoilainn wasn't a bitch for once, probably because I had a giant drach with me. Odhran and Niamh hugged me, promised they would watch for Ameline, too, and we were away again.

Oxford was in the dark when I stepped out of the veil into Femke's office. She shrieked, hands against her heart, before sagging a little, coming to my side.

"Sydlynn Hayle," she said as her arms went around me. "You scared me the rest of the way to death, you brat child."

I laughed, let her go. "I take it you felt a moment of magicklessness not so long ago?"

Femke shuddered, sank to the edge of her desk, eyes traveling over Max. "We won?"

I nodded, smirked. "Just hunting down a loose thread," I said as the door to her office opened.

Piers's smile almost split his face in half as he hugged me, too. At this rate, I was going to be all squeezed out before too long. It was hard to hold my resentment against him, despite the fact he forced me to abandon Quaid.

The Zornovs.

Sigh.

"Rescued me again, did you?" His fingers traced down my cheek. "I would have stayed and helped you."

"How are Ellis and the girls?" I really had to do better with names.

"Recovering," he said. "They're alive because of you." He hesitated. "Quaid and the others?"

It felt good to punch him in the arm. "Fine, too," I said. "And necessary, as it turned out. So you're forgiven for being a jackass."

He winced. "Nice you've forgiven me," he said. Shrugged. "Mum will get over it."

I grinned and hoped she found a suitable punishment. Because, you know. He needed the discipline. Didn't he?

"I'm just checking in, and letting everyone know we're good." I backed into Max. "And that if anyone stumbles on Ameline Benoit before me and does her any harm, they'll have me to answer to."

Femke saluted as Piers nodded.

The veil welcomed us one more time.

This is wishful thinking, isn't it? I sent the message to Max as the fear I was just chasing my own tail finally surfaced. *She's escaped. And I couldn't free my grandmothers.*

It wasn't until I parted the veil to Demonicon I understood.

And that fear went away in a gush of excitement when Ahbi hugged me the moment I touched the edge.

She tore the way open for me, left the gap wide as Max and I entered Meira's office. My sister squealed like a little kid, racing around her desk to engulf me in her embrace while our demon grandmother's spirit joined the massive hug with her own magic.

"What?" I turned to find her standing beside me, wavering in amber fire. Feeling almost as real as if she'd still been alive. "How?" Nice. Way to complete sentences and be all coherent, Hayle.

But Meira seemed to understand, Ahbi, too.

Free, Ahbi sent.

"There was a power drain," Meira said, breathless, cheeks redder than normal, "and I thought the Node was going to collapse." Her voice rose in excitement, a true storyteller. "And then, the power rushed back and, when I reached for the veil, Grandmother was back again."

Which meant Ameline wasn't maji anymore. Which meant no matter what she tried, she was no match for me.

Perfect.

Ahbi's form smiled at me.

Just before my sister punched me in the shoulder, so hard I staggered back in to Max.

"Don't you ever," she scowled, eyes blazing fire, "do anything that stupid again."

I rubbed my arm. "You're welcome," I said.

"I would have let her have my power," Meira said, softer this time. "You didn't have to ask Grandmother." Her eyes turned to Ahbi. "She's already given up so much."

Damn it. Made me think of Gram.

She had to do that, didn't she?

"Everyone's safe and sound," I said, excitement returning with evil delight as its bestie. "And I now understand why I couldn't track Ameline in the veil."

Meira's eyes flew wide. "You can do that?"

Couldn't resist. I poked the tip of her nose with my finger and winked. "I can."

Turned on Max. "Now I know what we're looking for."

He simply nodded, though wouldn't meet my eyes. "Then we must go," he said.

The least he could do was be happy for me. I was about to kill Ameline, crush her like a very disgusting bug scuttling under my feet now that she'd lost her maji abilities..

Unfair fight? So the hell what. Don't judge me.

This time when I entered the veil, it was under my power, with Ahbi sending me on my way in a hug of demon fire. But when I went looking for Ameline minus my grandmother's spirit, my heart almost stopped.

Wilding Springs called one last time as I retraced Ameline's path. Home? No. Please, let me be in time to stop her. I stepped out in to my back yard, on alert, running for the house, for Gram's room.

Empty. Though the house wasn't. I felt Mom, Sassafras, Shenka, dashed for the kitchen, terror building in me.

Only to find them all sitting there, around the table, coffee cups half raised, Gram making pancakes.

Gram.

Making.

Pancakes.

Even better?

Pink fuzzy socks graced her skinny feet.

For a moment, I was sure, so sure. Ameline was gone, had lost it all, down to the bare bones and Gram was whole, just like Ahbi.

But the truth hit me as I reached for my grandmother, felt her as reduced as ever.

I skidded to a halt, bursting into tears as I understood I'd still failed her.

Only to have her smack me with the spatula.

"What are you doing here?" She poked me with a sharp fingernail. "Where's that handsome husband of yours? If I'd known, I would have made more pancakes."

Sob. I hugged her, felt her free hand flutter against my back. When I pulled away, Gram's faded blue eyes were as watery as mine.

"Tell me about Demetrius," she said. "Is he...?"

"Fine," I said, wondering why she cared. Had they grown close since Gram lost her magic? He at least held great compassion for her. Gram sagged a little, nodding. "Chasing down some bad guys. Ass kicking." I grinned. "Whole again, jiggity jig."

She gasped, did a little dance. "Really?" Her hand fell, squeezed my arm. "You go find that little bitch," she said, "and you kill her once for me, okay then?" Gram turned back, singing off key as she flipped breakfast with a toss of one heel behind her in a show of joy.

No loss. Fate was wrong. Or, in making the right choice, I'd saved Gram.

What could be more perfect than that?

Destroying Ameline, of course.

More hugs, for Mom, Shenka, Sassafras and then, the veil.

One last try. I felt it in my bones.

But I didn't get a chance. Not yet. Not when I felt his power in the back yard, knew who still waited for me, Enforcer magic calling.

Not the same. But close enough.

I turned to Max, patted his arm. "Just give me a minute," I said, heading for the back door. "Try the pancakes."

And ignored the sad looks from my family as I forced air into my lungs before walking the length of the back hall and out into the late afternoon.

Quaid's Enforcer robe hung open, black death-metal t-shirt showing through, his big hands tightly clenched, driven in two balls of tension into the front pockets of his jeans. But when he saw me, he uncoiled, relief crossing his handsome features, chocolate eyes full of happiness.

"You're back," he said. Bit his lower lip as his head ducked, shoulders shaking, both hands lifting to cover his face.

I went to him, hugged him, let him lean against me, welcomed his magic, his scent into my world, offered him what comfort I could as he wept in my arms.

When Quaid finally backed away, he swiped at his wet cheeks with the shoulders of his robe, not meeting my eyes, chest heaving for air.

"I wanted to apologize," he said. Coughed softly. "To tell you I'm happy for you. If you're happy."

"I am," I said, without hesitation. Truth. "And you," I said. "Being an Enforcer. And Payten." Didn't hurt as much as it should have. That was a good thing.

Quaid hesitated. Shrugged. "I wanted you to know I'm here to help, whatever you need."

I probably should have been sad, but I couldn't bring myself to sorrow, smiling at him instead. "I'm looking for Ameline," I said. Held out one hand on impulse. "Want to come along for the ride?"

He took my offer without hesitation, our power linking, though in a new way, without the deep, abiding connection I was used to. Yes, the destiny we shared was still there, but the maji power I commanded made it easier. And, as he stood there with his heart in his eyes, I saw the thread keeping us together as a living thing.

And knew I could break it if I wanted to.

Selfish, I left it intact. Promised myself as I led him toward the house, I'd sever it later. That Ameline had to come first.

Almost ran into Max as he emerged from the back door, grasping my arm in his hand, eyes on Quaid and, without warning, pulling us both into the veil.

chapter thirty one

I hung onto Quaid as we spun into the veil, ready to smack Max for the lack of warning, only to have him stop, his power holding me in place.

Syd, he sent. *My task is at hand. And I beg you, forgive me.*

The veil tore open before I could ask him what the hell he was talking about. Max's magic shoved me through, his physical form following after.

I hit the ground hard, going down on one knee, bracing myself with both hands, breathless as Shaylee's Sidhe power connected with the earth magic of the Gate cavern. What the hell were we doing back here?

Quaid touched down beside me, a breath of air blowing past his lips from the rough landing. I started to stand, reaching for his hand to pull him up beside me.

Felt the groan of the cavern's power. The ache of its agony.

Turned in slow motion to see Ameline. Standing over Liam.

With blood on her hands.

And the shimmering form of Cian standing beside my fallen husband.

I choked, unable to act for the long, aching moment it took for Ameline to bend in a swift motion and plunge her hand into Liam's chest.

The source of the blood.

Oh.

My.

A part of my brain exploded, maji power moving forward toward her in a super nova flare of death so violent it was likely the entire cavern would collapse.

Didn't care.

Didn't.

Care.

Couldn't.

Breathe—

My power met a wall. Fate's wall, the same damned one, holding me back, keeping me from—

From Liam. From saving my husband.

My power sighed into nonexistence while Ameline laughed.

Fate.

No.

Please.

I'm sorry for your loss, Fate's voice echoed in my head. *But it is necessary.*

"My traitor of a Sidhe soul ran like the coward she is when the veils closed," Ameline snarled, drowning out Fate with her spiteful hate. "I need a new one." She stood, hands dripping crimson, blood magic, creation magic, coming to her call as she turned to Cian, the part of him Liam carried—

had carried

—fighting the sheath of red power imprisoning him.

She tried this before. Failed. The souls inside her almost killed her. Why did she think she would succeed this time?

More fury, red hot, blazing with demon fire, with as much hate as she focused on me.

"I'm going to eat your heart when I tear it out of your chest." Again I lashed at her.

Again my power fizzled out, lost, unused, falling against the wall as though it had never been.

Nononononononono.

NO.

Ameline stepped toward Cian, one of her hands going to her robe, pulling out a gun. Blood dripped from the tip as the thick stuff ran down her skin, the length of the barrel, gathering into a thick drop to fall in slow motion. The crimson splatter landing in the middle of Liam's forehead.

"I'll kill him," she said.

Giving me hope she'd wish she hadn't.

Alive. He was alive?

Liam was still alive.

"We should be working together," she spit her words at me like sharp edged weapons, "joined together. The planes would be ours. Even Fate wouldn't be able to stop us."

Quaid tried, too, struck with his Enforcer magic, only to have the ball of blue light sizzle and fall into helpless sparks feet from Ameline.

"Is that what he told you? Your Fate?" I felt Quaid move away from me, Ameline ignoring his attempt to attack her as if he wasn't there. My eyes flickering to follow, saw him kneel next to the dark, furred shape of Galleytrot.

Silent on the stone floor.

For the second time. And because of her.

My gaze snapped back to the muzzle of the gun, to Liam's pale face. Surely, Fate would let me deflect the bullet if she pulled the trigger? I reached for the weapon, felt my power retract yet again. The wall intact. Blocking me from Ameline.

From Liam.

Please, I screamed into the silence of my mind, toward Fate. *I'll do anything. Just save him.*

"We'll do a better job, don't you think?" Ameline's

laugh came out high-pitched, false and weak. "Than those foolish sorcerers. Than those who think they control things." The hand holding the gun shook, quivered as she plunged her free one into the red mist surrounding Cian. I heard him cry out through my connection to the Sidhe cavern, but I couldn't worry about him. Not while Liam lay bleeding.

He might not be dead yet, but he would be if I couldn't get to him. Stop the blood flowing from the hole in his chest.

So.

Much.

Blood.

Choke.

"I'll rule all of it one day," Ameline said. "But it would be easier if you were beside me." I almost didn't recognize what I was seeing in her, feeling from her. My focus on Liam was so intent I nearly missed it. But when I looked up at the crackle of need in her voice, my heart froze into a shard of ice.

Was that need in her eyes, longing? What was she looking for from me?

Sick and twisted, did she want me to love her?

Rejection formed a sphere of bile in my gut, coming out in my voice as I spoke. "I will never, ever stand with you," I said. "You are alone, Ameline. And you always will be."

She trembled, icy eyes losing their desperation a moment, turning to grief so profound I wondered what I'd done. Until her face returned to its monstrous rage and hate and her finger closed on the trigger.

"Then I will make it my life's mission," she hissed, "that you will be, too."

In that moment, I felt Fate's wall fall, knew this was part of my destiny, that I had a choice to make, saw Ameline's finger tighten even as Cian crumpled under her touch.

Go after Ameline. Or save my husband.

No brainer. Had to be Liam.

But the moment my magic struck the gun, more power blocked me.

Gaping in disbelief, I looked up and into Max's eyes as he stepped between me and my dying husband.

"Forgive me," he said.

What? No. Nofreakingwaynoabsolutelynot.

This. Was. Not. Happening.

I'd felt panic. Terror. Fury so vast I was sure it would consume me. But never had I felt such a need to act as I did in that moment. My power roared, gale-force winds behind it, slamming into Max's chest.

He swayed, face flinching.

But he held.

Again. Again I hit him, low, high, throwing every single ounce of power I had at him.

Max bent like a willow tree.

But he held.

Giant, painful sobs tore a hole in my chest, bigger than me, than the power I bore, bigger than the veil and the planes and all the magic in the Universe. I threw my body at him, feet impacting his stomach, his knees, hands pounding against his chest.

Max wept.

But he held.

While Ameline laughed.

I lifted my eyes from the immobile drach, watched, heart dying, as Ameline jerked Cian's power into her, devoured him. Her ice blue eyes flared green, mouth twisted in a terrible smile.

Blackness pooled at her feet, reached for my husband. Swallowed him slowly in a coating of hungry slime. No gunshot, not while Ameline ate Liam's soul along with his Sidhe's.

Desperation overwhelmed me, pushed me forward to hang from Max as he held me back, one arm reaching past him, for Liam.

As Ameline flickered into vampire shadow and vanished.

Gone. Taking the shattered pieces of my love with her.

I staggered back from the drach, looked up into his eyes. Saw his sorrow running deep, as ancient as he was.

"You asked Ameline's fate," he said. "She has now completed it."

"You killed him," I said, swaying where I stood. I felt Quaid's hands on me, pulled free. "Don't touch me." Shaking fingers rose, brushed at the tears on my face in absent strokes.

Please.

No.

Take me instead.

Max's big body moved aside, clearing the path for me. The press of his power keeping me from Liam had fallen, probably when Ameline left. Because Fate was a bitch.

How to bear such betrayal? My feet shuffled over the stone floor as the Sidhe cavern wept, its power rippling in answer to Liam's loss. The black pool was gone, his life stolen, as she'd taken Gram.

As she'd tried to take everyone I loved.

Da-dum.

What? My body stilled in an instant, entire being listening, the soft sound echoing in my chest.

Da. Dum.

A... heartbeat?

Liam.

Wild hope as powerful as any stray magicks threw me forward, on my hands and knees, pulling his head into my lap, while my egos dove inside him, searching.

Da. Dum.

His heart. Still beat.

Still.

Oh, Liam.

I reached for him, for the soul I loved, begged and screamed in the darkness, gave up everything to find him as I had to try to save him, the full weight of my maji power rushing forward into the black.

A tiny spark of life answered. So small and frail and fragile I cocooned it in my magic, cradling it to me even as I felt his chest lift under my hands, blood running once again from the ragged wound in his chest.

It won't stop, my vampire sent, as though through gritted teeth.

Flame sizzled, amber fire scorching the edges of the wound as Liam moaned.

And more blood flowed, endless, over my hands, over his thin white t-shirt, onto the stones, soaking through the knees of my jeans. I sucked in the blood power, tried to seal the hole Ameline left behind.

I'm only making things worse. My demon backed off, panting. *She's done something to him.*

Yes. Of course. The sorcery. Gram felt like this, Galleytrot, last time she attacked him. As though a vital part was being drawn away, devoured.

By her sorcery.

My own blossomed beneath me, maji power breaking apart at last. I let my own emptiness touch Liam, felt for her touch. Found it.

Crushed the connection.

His body sighed beneath my hands, her evil laughter echoing in my head.

I gasped through my sobbing as hazel eyes flickered open.

And his lips parted.

"Beautiful," he said in his last breath.

And died.

I felt him go, clung to him with everything I had, but it wasn't enough, would never be enough.

His spirit rose, blew me a kiss and vanished in a flash of light.

Leaving me to huddle over the empty shell he left behind.

CHAPTER THIRTY TWO

It took me a moment to realize I wasn't crying anymore. Not that I cared. Numb hollowness welcomed me into its embrace, the world around me only peripheral, uninteresting.

All but the feeling of his skin, now loose and cooling under my hands, the floppy way his head fell from my lap, face turning away as his empty hazel eyes stared off into nothing. How his blood felt chilly through my jeans, no matter how much my majiness kept me from sensing temperature.

Shivering, I hugged myself, hands wet with blood, wiping at a stray hair as it clung to the corner of my lip. Knowing I'd left a trail of him behind on my cheek.

Liam.

My darling Liam.

My oak tree was dead and nothing else mattered.

Two days, two nights. I looked down at the diamond on my hand, coated and glistening with crimson, amazed it was steady, no more trembling. Wow. Awesome. Wasn't it awesome I wasn't shaking anymore?

Sidhe power brushed against me, full of sorrow. My eyes lifted from Liam's empty face, met a black gaze simmering with red coals. A thick, wet tongue ran over my cheek, over Liam's blood, as Galleytrot flopped to his side, panting, weak. I felt him, recognized Ameline's touch, like it had been on Liam. Her hold on Galleytrot, the drain of his power, broken when I freed my love from her trap. And sent Liam into death.

But the big hound's heart remained as shattered as mine. The black dog lifted his head and howled his grief into the quiet of the cavern.

The world wobbled slightly as I sat back, feet sliding out from under me. Over blood, right? Yes, that was blood, slick on my sneakers. But whose blood?

Oh. Right.

I had to tell Liam to clean up after himself. Or Ameline maybe. This was her mess.

Um.

Wow.

Was this what it felt like to lose it?

Someone bent next to me, gentle, strong hands pulling me to my feet. I knew that chocolate magic, the heat of his power, but he was an Enforcer now. Why was

Quaid here? Liam was going to be pissed—

The family magic shuddered. My egos joined it, shaking me, screaming at me as my mind turned toward them, realized then they'd been calling for me. But why? What did they want?

Why was Quaid leading me away? Where were we going?

Giant feet came into view, long legs, huge hands. My eyes traveled up, massive chest, thick neck, bald head. Diamond eyes.

And the world snapped back into sharp focus.

His tears were the color of liquid mercury, his cheeks sheathed in the thick fluid, scales appearing as he grieved. Max held out one hand to me as Quaid stopped, still holding me up, and I stared at the drach.

"And this," he whispered in his deep, vibrating voice. "This was *my* Fate."

I nodded. Drew a breath.

And my power.

And hit him as hard as I could. One last time. So he would know.

That I would never, ever forgive him.

Or Fate.

Max staggered this time, going down to one knee, head bowed as I stood over him. My shaking was back, but I welcomed it, and the rage and heartbreak fueling it. The numbness whispered at the edges of my mind, begged me to retreat, to fall into quiet and the well of nothing, free of memory.

But my anger wouldn't let me.

I wouldn't let me.

Max knelt there for a long time before standing. As though waiting for me to kill him.

Tempting.

Better to make him live with what he'd done.

He turned, the veil opening beside him, and left without a word. Only the sound of Galleytrot's soft whimpers remained.

"Syd." Quaid's voice spun me around. His hands had blood on them too, like mine. From touching me. I looked down at myself, the gore covering my shirt, my jeans. My arms slick with my dead husband's blood. Looked back up and met his dark eyes.

"Bet you're glad you didn't marry me now, huh?" I waggled my eyebrows at him, voice falling from light and airy into a quavering half-cry.

Not funny. So. Not. But I laughed anyway, cracking around the edges again, even as my tears started and wouldn't stop.

The cavern suddenly flooded with people, Galleytrot allowing them inside the Sidhe cavern. Mom, Shenka, Sassafras. The coven. Charlotte. Piers and Femke.

So many. Who loved me.

Whom I couldn't bring myself to comfort.

259

I turned, left Quaid to answer their questions, sank back down to the floor at Liam's side. Smoothed his hair from his forehead, gently closing his hazel eyes. Kissed him once, on the lips.

And collapsed in a wretched heap of tears.

chapter thirty three

So weird, this image of me reflected back from the mirror. Three days ago, I'd worn white. Smiled, laughed, danced. Married a sweet, caring man who loved me with all his heart and never once asked anything of me but to be my husband.

To be my life.

And I said yes. I do. Accepted all he had to offer.

Selfish. Heartless. Put him in the line of fire.

And now, I sat in the same spot, with the same dazed look on my face. Only this dress was black.

I'd felt like an angel the day of my wedding.

I understood now, I had been.

Of death.

Three nights since I first wore his wedding ring. One since he died. And tonight, I readied to send my husband to his funeral pyre.

I smelled smoke on me already, but not some evil anticipation rising, no. This scent was real. I'd just been to another burning, hadn't I? Fate, the bitch, made sure Liam's funeral happened the same day they sent Mia to the stake.

It was still a struggle to know how to feel about other people. The numbness I'd almost allowed to carry me away in the Sidhe cavern offered continual comfort, taking the sharpness from my emotions and, for now, I permitted such intrusion, such softening of my terrible pain.

And my egos, they agreed with me, still and dull themselves, resting, sleeping, burying themselves in the dark quiet numbness offered. I could still sense them there, knew I wasn't alone. They would never allow me to feel abandoned, not now. But their grief was almost as comforting as the numb, knowing how much they missed Liam, Shaylee most of all.

Just as much as I did.

Mom hadn't wanted to tell me about Mia's trial. I only found out thanks to Charlotte who stormed into my room that very morning, fury on her face as Shenka and Mom tried to hold her back.

"You have to go," Charlotte said.

It was hard to raise my head, to feel interest, but her anger brought me back to a place where I could nod and listen and not be hollow.

"There are certain things you must see through to the end," my werefriend said, taking my hand, pulling me to my feet. "He would want you to be there when Mia dies."

He?

Oh.

My dead husband, Liam.

That was how I thought of him, privately. My dead husband, Liam. Couldn't shake it from my mind, the phrase trailing after me, poking me with a stick, don't forget. Always remember.

My dead husband, Liam.

Charlotte's hands grasped my arms, shook me a little. "Mia needs you," she said. "And you need to be there."

"Of course," I said, coughing to clear my throat. My dead husband, "Liam would want me to go."

The despair on Mom's face flashed only for a moment as I turned to her. "Why are they killing her today?" As in, why are you wearing that blouse? I like it, but it's a bit much, don't you think?

Sydlynn, my vampire sent. *It's time to rise.*

My demon grumbled. *Not yet*, she sent. *Let the girl burn. She betrayed us, didn't she?*

She was betrayed long before we met her, Shaylee sent, soft, with more caring than I could muster. *And she was our friend.*

Awareness, acceptance. I pulled away from the numb and smiled at Charlotte, just a little. Kissed my mother's cheek.

"I'm coming," I said. "Mia may have done horrible things, but she deserved to be loved. Even now, in the end."

Mom nodded, heavy and slow, hugged me. I pulled away quickly with a gasp of air.

Couldn't let her hold me for long. Her touch drove the numb away, made everything real again.

My dead husband, Liam.

I dressed in witch clothes, a midnight blue velvet skirt and pale blue silk blouse Shenka laid out for me. Left my hair down, face without makeup. Only the pentagram necklace around my neck.

And my rings, still on my left hand.

Two Enforcers came to fetch me and I allowed them to carry me, rather than going into the veil. Part of me dreaded it, the touch of the rubbery membrane, Ahbi's sorrow, the memories surfacing into spikes of flaming agony—

I knew neither of the Enforcers, thanked Mom for that in silence as I took a seat at the back of the Council hall. Shenka sat beside me, thigh against mine, hand reaching out to grasp my fingers in a gentle grip.

Looked down at my rings. Turned the bands. A flake of blood fell from the setting of the diamond, settling on my skirt.

Liam's.

The urge to pull away from the world was so powerful, my vision swimming with moisture, I could barely stand it. Liam's blood. On me still.

On my hands.

Until Shenka spoke, soft and private, in my ear, bringing me back again.

"They've fast-tracked Mia's trial," she said. Ah. The trial. Yes. Perfect. Talk about anything but...

My dead husband, Liam.

My left hand stroked over the velvet of my skirt, brushing the flake and the memory away even as a flare of demon fire cleaned the diamond to bright sparkle.

Diamonds reminded me of the drach. Of Max. Fate. Betrayal.

"Miriam tried to slow the proceedings, but the Council insisted." I clung to Shenka's fingers, my anchor to here and now. Hers tightened a little in response. "They've grown bolder and less willing to hesitate since the attack on the stronghold and the passing of conclave."

At least something good came of it.

And yet. Mia was going to burn today while they'd allowed Ameline months and months.

I couldn't think of her, either. Of her need for love, her twisted, damaged, ugly need for me to join her, to be like her.

Not yet.

"You probably know the Enforcers found Mia in the same cell where they held you captive, under guard of the drach."

Max.

No.

No thinking.

Later with the thinking. And the plotting revenge.

Shenka hissed. I looked down at her fingers, pressed tightly together, eased my grip. She didn't pull away, just kept going.

"Evidence was presented last night," Shenka said as the room filled with witches. I kept my eyes on the floor, though I could feel the pressure of their gathered magic, their sympathy. Layered more and more shielding over myself.

Almost welcomed the numb so I didn't have to feel at all.

"This morning is sentencing," Shenka said as the gathered witches rose as one, me slow beside my second, as the Council entered, took their seats. "There's little doubt what they will pronounce."

I finally looked up, met Mom's eyes across the room. She looked away first as her nasty little secretary unfurled a scroll, his words writing in the air next to him as he spoke.

"And so does the sentencing of Mia Rachelle Dumont commence."

Someone snickered, clear in the following quiet. I turned my head, saw Jean Marc and Kristophe staring at me.

Laughing and whispering.

Looked away.

Let them have their childish fun.

My dead husband, Liam, would have been pissed, though.

They led her in, then, my old friend, between two Enforcers, her emaciated body draped in a thin, white gown. I'd worn one just like it, the memory of the feeling of it sharp and crisp, as though I still had it on. Reached up and touched the sleeve of my blouse just to check.

So. Real.

And so unreal. Mia looked around her, beaming smile and icy blue eyes full of happiness. Excitement. She clapped her hands as the two Enforcers left her in the middle of the central podium.

"For me?" She said, twirling to look at all the witches watching. "I've always wanted a surprise party."

Gone, she was gone, and I'd done it to her, hadn't I? My maji power erased her memory, gave her a childhood she'd never known, innocence she'd never been allowed.

And yet, here we were. About to kill her anyway.

"Mia Dumont," Mom said. "You stand accused of joining forces with the Brotherhood, giving over knowledge and power to them, betraying all witches, all magic races in your attempt to steal the power of the Dumont family coven."

Mia wasn't looking at Mom. She hummed softly to herself, twirling side to side with her robe in her hands, flaring the bottom out over her feet.

Sweet.

Sad.

How could I bear it?

Mom's sigh was visible, audible as she looked up and down the line of witches on the Council.

"We're certain?"

Immobile as mountains, those angry faces. And those of the watchers. They hated her, it was clear to me, didn't care she had no choices, no hope, no life beyond the lie she lived for her first eighteen years. The pain and suffering she endured in that time and the years after. The broken soul she tried so hard to mend.

Mom met my eyes again. And spoke.

"Mia Dumont," Mom said, voice heavy with regret, "for the crimes you have been proven guilty of, this Council sentences you to burn at the stake until you are dead, your bones crushed and scattered so never again can your echo be called, nor your magic added to the rolls of your family coven."

Mia looked up, then. Smiled at Mom. "You're so pretty," she said.

They led her away while Shenka held my shaking

hand. I stood, freed myself of my second's grip, pushed through the crowd of staring, whispering witches. Hopped over the last row of chairs with a boost of power.

And went after Mia.

Not one soul tried to stop me.

I found her in a small, white room just outside the Council door, the same two Enforcers guarding her. They didn't comment, stepped aside to let me through. I had no idea what I intended to accomplish going to see her.

I only knew I had to.

Mia looked up from where she sat on the edge of the small wooden cot pushed into the far corner of the room. Her smile lit the spare, terrible space with its joy as she stood and came to me.

Hugged me.

Kissed my cheek.

And frowned in concern, murmuring comfort to me as I began to weep.

Mia led me to her bed, sat me next to her. Cradled me against her while she rocked me gently and stroked my hair.

"There, there, sweet girl," she said. "Everything's going to be all right."

I pulled away, met her eyes, lower lip trembling uncontrollably. "Will it?" The numb tried to take me, and I wanted it to so much. But Mia's soft, steady gaze, her sweet smile, the way she stroked my hair back from my cheek before gently patting my hand, made me want to stay.

With her. For a while.

"Did you know," Mia said, giggling softly, "I think one of my bodyguards really likes me." She rolled her eyes, batted her lashes. "He's cute. Maybe he'll ask me out when the party is over."

"Maybe." I snuffled, wiped my nose on the corner of my skirt. "Mia, do you remember me?"

"Of course I do, silly." She gave me a gentle push. Then frowned a little. "I do know you, don't I? From somewhere?"

My head felt like it held up the weight of the world as I nodded. "I'm Syd," I whispered.

She laughed. "Syd." Hugged me. "Of course you are."

Choke.

Unbearable, this final heartache.

And then the door opened, and Quaid stood there.

I was wrong. There was so much more pain to come.

Mia clapped her hands, motioned for him to join us. Winked at me so broadly I realized this was the Enforcer she'd been talking about. She'd forgotten her own brother.

I sometimes joked I was going to hell.

This time, I really believed it.

He took her hand, helped her to her feet. Mia kissed

his cheek with a girlish giggle before sinking back to the bed and pressing her face into my shoulder, blushing. I watched Quaid's face crumple in sorrow, able to understand the depth of his loss.

Reached for his hand. Took it in mine when he accepted.

Shared his loneliness as his sister smiled at both of us.

"Maybe I'm wrong," she whispered to me. "Maybe it's you he loves."

Quaid dropped my hand, looked away as I forced a smile, surely the barest of expressions, and hugged her.

"Maybe," I whispered back. "But I don't think so."

Quaid's shoulders slumped when the door creaked and one of the guards entered.

"They are ready," the Enforcer said.

I wasn't. Not now, not yet. Not ever.

Mia stood, spun in a circle before reaching out her arms to the waiting Enforcer.

"It's going to be the grandest party ever," she said. Hooked her arm through his.

And followed him out into the courtyard on the other side.

I stayed where I was, unable to stand, legs powerless beneath me, though my tears were dried, my ability to cry gone, washed away with her departure.

Quaid sat next to me, fingers laced, elbows on his knees.

When he offered his hand, it was my turn to accept. We sat there for a long time while the courtyard filled, the sound of voices carrying into the small room, until I couldn't bear to listen.

He rose as though to some silent call to action, me beside him. Walked out into the sunshine, still holding my hand.

We stood, side by side, as Mia was tied to the stake in the center of the platform, smiling, waving until her hands were bound at the gathered witches come to watch her die. When the Enforcers stepped back, she met my eyes, a single tear trickling down her face.

Was her awareness returning?

No. Not now. I couldn't let her suffer ever again.

My maji power reached for her, soothed her. Sang a song of peace and love to her, a song I thought I'd forgotten. Her smile returned just as her head sagged to one side and Mia fell into slumber.

And no one, though they turned to stare, called me out.

Not even Andre Dumont. He had what he wanted. His scowl told me he didn't approve. I showed him an image of himself burning, saw him flinch away from me.

And had no doubt I'd find a way, one day, to make what I'd shown him reality.

For Mia.

Mom stepped forward, blue flame falling from her

hands into the piled kindling. They rose in a roar, in haste, devouring everything so quickly I knew, even without my maji help, Mia would have felt no pain.

I forced myself to watch my friend, the fire devouring her body in a blast of heat. I shielded Quaid from the overwhelming temperature as the rest of the watching witches fell back, so he could stay with his sister until the very end.

It was over quickly, Mom's magic force-feeding the coals into death so, in a matter of minutes, only ash and white bones remained.

Her last act filtered Mia's skeleton from the black and crushed it into dust.

Quaid shuddered, turning his head toward me, face wet with tears.

And then, the most remarkable thing. She rose from the ash, the most beautiful girl, her long, black hair shining in the sunlight, blue eyes bright with joy. No longer a withered mess as she'd gone to her death, the soul of Mia Dumont floated free, egoless, ghostly echo gone with the crushing of her bones.

I knew it was her spirit hovering there. Felt the purity of it, that she was ready.

And waved, smiling and crying as she blew me a kiss before hugging herself. Tipping her head to her brother.

Flashed into a blaze of multi-colored light.

Free.

The witches left, some of them finally feeling remorseful, the Council's power humming low with Mom's regret. She didn't interfere when Quaid stayed behind, let us be when I hugged him, cried with him as much as comforted him.

But when we pulled apart and he reached up to touch my face, I flinched back.

Knew what he was about to say. To offer.

And just couldn't accept.

"I'll be okay," I said. Felt it now, the truth. Thanked Mia for her gift in the end. She knew all along.

Everything was going to be all right.

He let me go, hand sliding from mine as I turned and went to Shenka.

Reached for the veil and home.

I shivered from the memory of Mia's death, returning to the present at last. I dropped my eyes from the sunken-gazed woman in the glass, slid my hands over the stiff, black fabric of my dress.

Flinched at the knock on my door.

Mom came inside, didn't touch me, held her distance.

"It's time," she said.

chapter thirty four

The Council had restored the old coven site with magic after the closing of conclave. I was happy to see the trees back in their places, the grasses growing high again in the periphery. The old pentagram was gone, our house now the center of the family's power. But this location still had great meaning for the coven and seemed the perfect place to send Liam on.

I considered burning his body in the Sidhe realm, but discarded the idea just as quickly. Liam was a Gatekeeper, but he was a Hayle. And this glade combined the best of both.

Mom released my hand as we stepped out of the veil into the clearing, the family already gathered and waiting for us. Ahbi's spirit was gentle, but didn't offer comfort.

Bless her for knowing I didn't want any just yet.

The sky had darkened to black, pinpoints of stars

sharing their light on this moonless night. Black robes parted, let me through, the family embracing me with their magic as Ahbi had done, but their sympathy held in check.

How well they knew me.

Gram waited in the center, Sassafras in her arms, Shenka beside her. Meira's cheeks shone with tears. Charlotte came forward, led me to stand with my grandmother before backing away, head down, hands folded.

The pyre waited, empty and cold, a stack of wood the size of a coffin, bare and open to the endless sky. I reached for Galleytrot, felt him answer, his power only beginning to recover from Ameline's attack, but more than enough.

More than enough to deliver my dead husband, Liam, to his final rest.

Mom hadn't wanted to allow me to prepare the body, but I didn't give her a choice. Arrived home from Mia's burning and locked myself in the Sidhe cavern with him. Chased out those she'd sent to deal with his mortal form. Phon and Lula Kennecott left immediately, bowing to me. The healer twins had washed him, laid him out on a table in a suit Mom must have provided.

I undressed him, trying not to register the stiffness of his limbs, thankful I barely felt the cold of his flesh. And slipped him into his favorite clothes. The white t-shirt I smoothed out over the thin bandage the twins used to cover his wound. His second favorite pair of jeans came next, the first gone, covered in his blood. Socks, sneakers. I tousled his hair, stroked his cheek.

Sat with him a while, holding his cold hand, willing warmth into it. Wishing I could go after him, knowing there was no hope. Bouncing between hate and love and desperate tears that came in waves I couldn't control.

Until Mom came, led me away to prepare myself for the funeral.

And I went with her. Left my darling there, the giant black hound collapsed at his side. Galleytrot never left him, not for a moment, mournful power hanging like a shroud around my dead husband.

My Liam.

And now, the faithful dog brought the body out, the hound of the Wild Hunt's glowing green power appearing through the veil I opened for him, guiding him without me through the labyrinth of the veil and out again, carrying Liam's form wrapped in a sheath of magic.

The family bowed their heads as Liam floated forward, settling softly on the pyre.

Disturbance, yelling, a slamming car door. I wasn't expecting this interruption, turned to find Sonja O'Dane forcing her way through the family, though their hands tried to hold her back, her Unseelie power sparking and flaring, slippery. Mom moved before I could, but too late, as Liam's mother stopped before me.

Slapped me across the face.

My head rocked to the side, blood heating the inside of my mouth. Stunned, on pause, I turned slowly back.

And met her furious eyes as Charlotte wrestled her away from me.

Sonja collapsed into my werefriend's arms even as Galleytrot approached with a rumbling growl.

"This is your fault!" Her power slapped me again, barely registering as her physical blow had. Shaylee shuddered, tried to fight back, but I held her off.

No. I had to hear this.

I deserved this.

"My son is dead." Sonja's hate bubbled forth, Liam's spell keeping her complacent and happy clearly broken. "And no one would let me near him. None of you!" She spun away from Charlotte, spit at my feet. "He's dead and you killed him and you didn't want me to know." She collapsed to her knees, shaking, sobbing, a wreck.

I knew how she felt. And couldn't bring myself to comfort her.

Because she was right.

Blue power flared overhead, two Enforcers appearing. Mom must have called them. I almost stopped her when she gestured to Sonja.

This was her son. Didn't she deserve the right to be here?

"Please escort Mrs. O'Dane to the other side of the pyre." Mom wasn't completely heartless then.

Sonja went, stumbling, falling, wailing her grief into the night as the two black-robed Enforcers did as they were ordered.

Mom's hand fell on my arm, pulled me around, tears on her cheeks.

"Sweetheart," she said.

I shook my head, looked at Liam lying in death on the pile of wood that would carry him away from me forever.

Why didn't I listen to Gram? To Sassafras? They were right. Liam wasn't strong enough.

And I wasn't. I should have kept him safe. Would Ameline even have gone after him if he wasn't mine?

Of course she would have, Galleytrot growled to me. *Except his last days would have been sad, in longing, instead of full of love and happiness.*

Small comfort, I sent.

Not for me. He came to my side, sat next to me, black eyes empty, leaning in with his furry shoulder. *And not for Liam.*

I stepped up to his body, slipped the rings from my finger. Laid them on his chest, kissed his cold cheek.

Finally stepped back, beside Galleytrot, his presence comforting, the feel of the earth and an approaching summer storm.

I raised one hand, set it on the dog's head. Scratched a

little. Nodded.

And set fire to the pyre.

I wished I'd see him rise again, just one more glimpse, though the memory of him doing so in the cavern was still with me. This time, though, I knew I wouldn't. Already asked Galleytrot. Turned out Sidhe didn't have echoes like witches did. And his spirit was long gone.

I watched the pyre flare and smoke, catch in a rainbow of flames as my egos joined me, my maji power feeding the heat until a trail of sparkling embers rose into the uncaring night.

Taking my dead husband, Liam, away from me.

chapter Thirty five

Trill was waiting for me at the kitchen table when we arrived home. Rose and came to me, hugged me.

"I'm sorry," she said. "I wish we could have been there to help."

She was the first one I'd allowed to say such a thing to me. Hit me like a slap across the face.

Sorry. She was sorry. They all were. I could feel it now, a blanket trying to smother me and, for a moment, I fought against it with all the energy inside me.

Not much left to fight with. Their need to comfort me finally won, the power of my family hugging me where once they felt like doom. Love seeping through until, at last, I shook myself and woke up.

And realized I wasn't broken, lost. Not anymore. I could handle their sympathy and sorrow. Didn't need the numb, after all.

I'd survived Liam's death.

Now I just had to survive living.

"You did everything you could," I said. Turned to Mom, Charlotte, Shenka, Gram. Meira. Sassafras with his drooping ears, Galleytrot, head low. "All of you. Thank you. But no one is to blame. No one but Ameline."

That's right, Syd. Better believe it.

I left them in the living room, talking, drinking tea and eating cookies Shenka whipped up in about five seconds. She followed me with a pair of steaming chocolate chip mounds on a napkin, but I turned on the stair, kissed her cheek, shook my head.

Went to my room.

I lay down, but couldn't sleep. My mind refused to stop, showing me the fire, Mia, Liam, winding them together, night and day and sun and starlight, blue flame, rainbow, Mia's smiling face, Liam's quiet.

I tried a hot shower, cursed softly into the steam as my body ignored the temperature I once adored. Paced and wrung my hands, going over and over what happened, wondering if there was anything I could have changed, done.

Forced myself to stop. Sit. Breathe.

The numb remained, waiting. Eager for me to embrace it.

I banished it with a sigh as my vampire's voice spoke in my head.

Why are we here? She prodded me gently. *There's somewhere else you'd rather be.*

My demon rumbled her agreement. Shaylee sighed in answer even as the family magic urged me up.

Up.

And to my door.

I slipped into the hall, felt for the sleeping minds surrounding me. Charlotte in my old room, still here. Trill and her brothers in the back yard, tucked into their rusting caravan. Mom in Shenka's room, my second on the couch.

Gram.

Easy to creep past them, down the steps, into the back yard. I paused by Gram's door, felt Sass sleeping, but knew she was wide awake. Felt me going.

Let me.

The night was oddly cool for August, my breath showing in front of me the only real indication. I could have ridden the veil easily enough, but I chose to walk instead, allowing the quiet of the darkness to swallow me whole and wash me clean.

Town Hall loomed in the distance, brick walls lit by cold florescence. I passed through the side door, the lock giving way under my fingers as I entered easily, as always. Familiar, this pilgrimage, filled with memory and expectation.

Down the hall to the back stairs. Into the basement.

Pausing by the wall where the Sidhe wards waited.

For Liam.

I gulped air, forced to bend over in half, hands on my thighs, to keep from dry heaving the wash of sudden grief gripping me. Panting, sweating from the effort, swallowing down bile begging for release, I pressed my forehead to the cinder-block wall and choked on air.

Pulled myself together.

Walked through the wards.

Galleytrot looked up, groaned softly as he saw me. Waited for me to cross to him where he lay before the Gate. I felt a tingle as I approached, knew who was calling from the other side. Shaylee opened the way, the big Gate's sorrow as real as mine as it slowly, slowly released and swung back.

Thalion stood in silence on the Sidhe side, a face so dear and familiar beside his I had to clap both hands over my mouth to keep from screaming.

Fergus, Liam's grandfather. Who looked so like my dead husband, Liam.

Sidhe had no empathy. And yet, Thalion's face showed his grief and I was grateful for that.

Fergus bowed his head to me. Held out one hand. "Syd," he said in Liam's voice. "He loved you so much."

I couldn't do this, not tonight. Staring into Liam's face, hearing his voice. And yet.

And yet.

When I let it, when I finally stopped fighting, seeing Fergus brought me the most comfort of all.

"We are now without a Gatekeeper." I could have hugged Galleytrot for the distraction.

Thalion nodded, sighed. "Truth," he said. "Liam O'Dane was the last."

My eyes met Liam's—Fergus's—again. "Can we have you back?" I tried a little smile, found it worked, my lips moved, turned up.

Amazing.

But Thalion shook his head. "He's too long in our realm now," he said. "His mortal form was already dying. Any attempt now for him to go back to your plane will end in his death."

I shivered. "Not going to happen," I said.

Galleytrot chuffed softly. "We could simply try to find a way to dispense with the knock." Every year, the Sidhe power called to the Gatekeeper. And every year he had to answer or the wall between our planes would fall and they would be one with us again.

Thalion's shrug was elegant, graceful. "It is part of the realm and not ours to control. But Sydlynn is maji," he said. "It is possible."

Okay, disaster averted. Maybe.

I'd deal with it later.

"I fear," Fergus said—oh, good, Syd, you called him Fergus—"you will need Cian to do so, Sydlynn."

Yet another reason to hunt down Ameline.

Like I needed one more.

Thalion bowed, Fergus waving as the Gate sighed shut again, leaving Galleytrot and I alone.

I sank to the stone floor as he stretched out beside me, head in my lap while I crossed my legs and leaned my elbow on my knee. My free hand stroked his soft ear, both of us staring at the Gate, lost in thought.

"Syd," Galleytrot whispered, "how can you forgive me?"

I looked down into his eye, a tiny ember of red burning in its depth.

"Silly dog," I said. "What's to forgive? You didn't hurt Liam."

"I failed to protect him." Galleytrot's eye closed, soft whine rising in his chest. "For the second time, she came and laid me low. And for the second time, Liam paid the price for my weakness."

I knew I didn't have a corner market on guilt or blaming myself. But I'd forgotten all about the big hound and just how badly he'd be feeling after Liam's death. I guess it was understandable, my lack of attention. But as I bent and hugged his big head, resting my cheek on his, I let him feel how I felt through a surge of magic.

"This is not your fault," I said. "Fate decided long ago." I thought of Max and the blind maji woman I now fought very hard not to hate. "There is always choice, but we are made to make them the way Fate designed."

Galleytrot sighed, a chest-heaving doggy sigh. "What are we going to do without him?"

"I don't know." The last word came out in a flood of tears, tears I quickly dashed, letting out a sigh of my own. "I'm too tired to think about it right now." More flickers of images, of Max, in particular. His betrayal hit me harder than I thought it would. Why? Maybe because I felt such a kinship to the drach.

Or maybe because I would never betray a friend.

Fate be damned.

And Mia's loss weighed on me, despite the fact I knew her spirit was free, happy. And with Liam's death, all layered on top of each other so quickly, right after victory was mine...

Bed.

Covers over head.

World go away.

Not a solution. But one I considered as I sat there with the sad hound whimpering like a puppy.

"Was any of it worth it?" Despair almost carried me away right there and then, the tears coming back with a vengeance. Would I never run out of them? Surely there was a moisture limit my body could tolerate, a point where they would dry up. Where I would.

Or risk crumbling to dust.

Galleytrot didn't answer, just reached for me with his

Sidhe power.

And a flare of heat reached back.

Just the barest point of light, but powerful nonetheless, stretching, warming me in the pit of my stomach.

No. Not my stomach.

I knew this heat, felt it the moment Liam and I said "I do". Had felt it again when we'd made love.

Understood it now as the tiny little life hummed its happiness inside me.

A soul, soft and kind and loving, budding with possibility.

Part of me. Part of Liam.

My tears flowed further, but this time with hope and happiness I never thought could come again. I burrowed my face into Galleytrot's fur, laughter bubbling, giggling out of me as he looked up, red fire flaring in his eyes.

I wiped at my face, drew a giant breath and let it out, sagging, hugging myself, rocking a little before I dropped my hands to grab his snout and kissed his nose.

"I don't think we'll have to worry about not having a Gatekeeper after all," I said.

Galleytrot's power held still, ears perked, body quivering.

"As long as the Gate is willing to wait nine months, that is."

He leaped to his feet, did a wild dog dance, front

paws clawing the air before he fell at my side again, joy glowing from every inch of him.

"Syd," he said.

I nodded.

And, as the little soul inside me sparked with growing life, my heart began to heal.

chapter thirty six

One thing was absolutely certain: Fate sucked.

And I couldn't wait to get a chance to tell her just how much.

Anger returned with the beginnings of my recovery. A lot of it. So much I worried about the nugget growing inside me, at times, and did my best to shield him from what how I felt.

Him. Yup. I guess I shouldn't have been surprised.

In the meantime, I decided to start with Max. Took a quick trip to Demonicon and the drach peak, only to find it empty.

And no amount of searching the veil turned up his traitorous ass or any of his people, either.

Just wait until I got my hands on his dragon hide.

As for Fate, the way to Center was closed to me. I could only imagine she was terrified I was coming to kick her scrawny ass all the way around the veil.

Sure, Syd. That was it.

Iepa's sorry little soul was hiding from me, too. Bunch of cowards.

If this was what it meant to be maji, ducking and covering while other people suffered? I'd have to find a new line of work because *hell* freaking *no*.

Just. No.

At least it was nice to see the empty plane flourishing at last. My trip to the stronghold to check for the drach turned into a happy moment of deep breathing in the scent of flowers and the freshest air I'd ever breathed.

Not so empty anymore.

The stronghold was happy to see me, sad for my loss, but excited and chatty about his own possibilities. I spent far longer with him than I intended, just soaking up happy.

I needed it, because this teetering between grief and joy wore me out.

And with the Enforcers back in control, I worried less about anyone—like Ameline—looking for a way to take advantage of the power still stored in the stronghold's heart. She might have Cian's soul inside her, but she was missing demon power yet, and with Ahbi on high alert and my sister sworn to Demonicon for the time being, Ameline's ability to become maji again had gone down the toilet.

Into the sewer. Where she belonged.

I worried I hadn't heard from Demetrius and searching for him proved fruitless, too. Yes, I could track people through the veil, but sorcery didn't leave much of a trail. Which meant Rupe and Belaisle evaded me, too.

I tried to trust the fact Demetrius was whole again and could take care of himself. Kind of tough to do these days. My sense of protectiveness for those I cared about had taken a giant leap into obsessive, so much Shenka had to sit me down and tell me to back off when the coven complained they couldn't take a shower without me poking my nose in.

Okay then. Sheesh.

Not like they weren't all up in my business.

Not exactly fair. They were kind and loving and made sure I was okay. Which I was. Most of the time. When I let myself stop and think about Liam, not so much. But the growing peanut in my belly went a long way to pulling me free of my funk.

The Brotherhood was pretty much non-existent these days, all the sorcerers the drach captured turning up imprisoned in the stronghold for the Enforcers to find. Mom and her Council Leader friends were ruthless. I stayed out of it.

I doubted they needed me around, suggesting violent means to kill the sorcerers.

Eva Southway did report a swell in recruitment to the

Steam Union, which made me nervous. Mom, too. What if the Brotherhood members—as I was sure they were—who remained outside the last battle were only seeding themselves inside the good sorcerer order?

Eva assured us both she was keeping a close eye.

Lot of good that would do if Liander Belaisle popped up out of nowhere and poked it out.

Still, none of my business. She made that clear to me before leaving Mom's Harvard office after assuring us she'd keep us posted.

Okay then.

My Ameline search came to an abrupt halt when Mom found out I was pregnant. I knew it was going to happen, did my best to hide the wee spark from her, but my mother was a master of deceit and trickery herself.

Grasped onto me the instant she uncovered the truth and refused—absolutely refused—to let me go.

And then betrayed me to the family. Shenka, Charlotte, Sassafras. And effectively pinned me to the ground with their focused attention.

Yes, I could have ignored their need for me to pull back, protect myself. But Mom made an excellent point.

If Ameline found out I was pregnant, we had no idea what she would do. Would she try to hurt the baby in an effort to hurt me?

Hurting her was one of my priorities. Naturally, I had nightmares of Ameline coming after my nugget.

Growl, snarl, howl.

Just. Let. Her. Try.

And so, I settled in to Wilding Springs after that, with my growing belly and my overprotective family hovering around me like I was going to spontaneously combust at any second.

And you know what? They were right. My son was the most important thing to me now. Even killing Ameline, even restoring Gram—as hard as it was for me to admit—nothing, no one came before my baby.

There would be time to rip her in half and drink her blood when my son—our son—was born.

Why wasn't I surprised how excited Sassafras and Mom were over the pregnancy? And, to my relief and happiness, Gram. The three of them followed me around in various pairings, worse after Mom relocated herself to the house for the duration of my gestation. The first time I felt them feeding the baby power, I laughed and opened to it.

Because, even though I knew they'd made me the way I was—all messed up and loyal and crap—and would do the same to my son, I knew they made me the way I was.

All messed up and loyal and crap.

And I wanted my son to have the benefit of their love.

Galleytrot was a bit of an issue, though. He literally glued himself to my side, sleeping next to my bed, furry body pressed against me when I walked anywhere, to the point I got tired of tripping over him and opened my mouth to tell him to back off.

Only to see the hope and need in his eyes.

And sighed. Let him be.

And accepted this wasn't just *my* son I was growing.

Honestly, the best part of this was seeing Gram blossom again, almost back to her old self. Even weakened, only a fraction of her power left, she bounced around the house like a kid, fuzzy socks firmly in place, hugs and kisses and smacks with her favorite spatula all making me laugh.

If she fed me one more pancake with the goal of "fattening me up for the baby," I was going to explode.

Liam's bones went to the Hayle family vault, safely stored there with my family. I didn't go with Mom when she interred him, choosing to remain at home, focused on the baby. Not because I didn't love him anymore, but because I wanted to remember Liam as I'd seen him last—in Fergus's smile.

My only moments of worry for the baby came when I felt the Sidhe power in him flare from time to time. But a quick check in with Thalion answered my fears about Cian and my baby's Sidhe soul. Had Ameline stolen it when she'd taken Liam's through some father/son connection? Turned out Cian split himself so long ago, there were parts of him in every Gate, in every

Gatekeeper. Which meant my child had his very own part of the Gate creator.

His Sidhe soul was safe.

My hitchhikers were hilarious, cooing and talking to the boy all the time. Shaylee was the worst, all smug how her Sidhe power connected to him so easily. I was happy to feel the other girls and the family magic linked with him only two months after he was conceived, as though it was meant to be that way.

Shaylee pouted briefly, but got over her exclusivity and went all happy auntie/alter ego again.

It was nice to hear from Sebastian after his transformation. He contacted me shortly after Liam's funeral to tell me how deeply sorry he was for my loss. Even as he did, I felt the breathless excitement in my vampire friend and was happy for him.

Sebastian was still trying to figure out what I'd done, how I'd changed him, but didn't regret a moment of it and left my mind with an embrace and a kiss of power that felt like me.

Piers showed up at the house about a week or so after—I started thinking in terms of before Liam and after Liam and wondered if that was normal—to share his sympathy, apologize a few more times, and reassure me his mother wasn't going to open up the Steam Union to disaster. I believed him over her and accepted his determination.

He was enough like me I knew he'd never let the Steam Union fall.

At least not without a massive fight.

Over the next few weeks, he continued to show up, finally offering to be there for me if I needed him. Sadly, but kindly, I finally sent him away.

Too soon, way too soon. And yet, I knew once my baby was born, I'd have to start thinking about it. Because a son, Liam's son, was a wonderful thing, but I really needed a daughter. Coven rules.

Sigh.

Piers left at last, once his offer was made, but only after telling me he'd traded posts with his sister, Clover, and was now in our territory full time.

Varity hovered, spending more time with Gram than ever, offering help so frequently I finally had to tell her in no uncertain terms she'd done as Fate demanded and to stop being a freak already. Worked. She hugged me, forgave herself. At least, didn't seem so desperate to prove her loyalty or make up for my loss.

Wasn't her job, anyway.

Charlotte spent more time with us, too, rather than her usual half time at home, bringing me baby clothes and cute toys, cooing to my belly in her wolf voice until I giggled. Made me wonder if she was considering the whole marriage thing in a new light.

Alison's disappearance and hopeful destruction made

me sad, though it probably shouldn't have. There was no sign of her, but I'd lost track of her before and failed to find her. Refused to just let it go in case she'd managed to survive after all.

She'd had the combined powers of Ameline and I pour through her. Who knew what that did to her if it didn't kill her at last?

Though those closest to me didn't approve, I spent every other night, as promised, sleeping in Liam's bed in the cavern, and the alternate at home, in mine. It was so hard to see the boxes set aside next to my closet, waiting for Liam to appear and unpack them, but it was months before I let Shenka take them away.

I guess I really wasn't ready to let him go, just yet.

His scent stayed a little while, but not as long as I would have liked. Mom finally showed up one night with Galleytrot and a set of fresh sheets, a new quilt.

It just wasn't the same after that.

But I understood. The cavern was so quiet now, just me and Galleytrot. And the nugget. I took a lot of comfort from the place, knowing how much Liam loved it, but knew, now his presence was almost completely gone, I'd have to move on. Especially since sleeping there made me cry every single night.

Had to be the pregnancy, right? All those hormones?

Sure, Syd. Sure.

I could blame it on the peanut. He didn't mind a bit.

Like what you read? Find out more at
pattilarsen.com

Here's a look at the first chapter of the final volume,
Book Twenty of the Hayle Coven Novels

the last call

CHAPTER ONE

I couldn't see my feet. Who was I kidding? Knees, either. Thing was, it was probably for the best.

Considering I'd blown up to the approximate size of a zeppelin on steroids with a healthy dose of hippopotamus thrown in for good measure, I was certain I wouldn't recognize my own feet even if I could lay eyes on them.

Grunt.

Everything was an effort. Walking. Standing. Talking. Breathing.

And if I had to pee one more freaking time, I was going to choke someone.

Lula Kennecut's smiling face appeared over the mound of giantness that was my belly, her healing magic retreating as she folded down the hem of my dress—affectionately referred to as the pup tent—and gently patted the nugget making my life miserable.

"You're doing amazingly well," she said, nose wrinkling as she helped me up, freckles scrunching across the bridge and out over her round cheeks. Her hazel eyes sparkled with good humor as she brushed back a stray lock of her brown hair, fallen loose from her pony tail.

"Thanks." Grunt. My bladder protested as I sat erect. Peanut's foot or hand or something hard pressed fiercely in every which direction. Including my spine. My liver. And, I was sure, any day now he'd find a way to tap-dance on all of my major organ at once.

That would be just delightful.

Grunt.

At least I was over my embarrassment. The first time Lula wanted to have a little look-see at some very private parts of mine, I almost freaked out. Almost. Now, I just wanted her to reach in there and take him out already.

Would have paid her.

"Can you tell if he's ready yet?" Mom hovered, smiling and twitching, one hand patting my shoulder, the other stroking my hair, but on autopilot. As though it wasn't me she soothed.

Sheesh.

Lula shrugged her thin shoulders, making me want to kick her. Hard. Somewhere painful.

"He'll come when he's ready."

I. Hated. Her. So. Much.

"We could just take him out now, right?" I tried to

stand, needing Mom to support me as I fought to rise from the edge of the bed. I immediately pressed both of my hands to the small of my back as the massive weight in front tried to sever my spinal cord in three places. My vertebra groaned in protest.

And women did this multiple times?

We were cracked.

Lula's power reached out, slid inside my back, eased the pressure until I sighed in relief and actually found I could smile after all.

She was kind of forgiven. For now.

The young healer took my hand in hers, massaging the palm with strong fingers, power radiating outward from her touch. "We could encourage him to come early," she said, "but part of his proper development is his own choice of freedom. I know you don't want to risk even a tiny detail when it comes to your son's birth."

Damned witches and our stupid magical needs. Unlike normal babies, ours had to be allowed to emerge on their own. Only in the most dangerous circumstances did witches have cesarean sections. Part of our power emergence came from the desire to be an individual, to be free.

Sucked so much. Besides, the nugget was more Sidhe than anything, right? And, from the feeling of him, as sweet and easy going as his father—

Choke.

I pushed down the flare of tears that rose when I thought about my dead husband, Liam—

Reached for irritation. There it was, waiting on the sidelines. My favorite.

"I know, I know." I grumbled as I shuffled away from Lula, heading for my door, my bare feet scuffing over the carpet. Mom and Lula followed me into the hall. Charlotte waited at the top of the stairs, already reaching for me as I neared the landing. The weregirl's very firm grip on my arm and stoic expression told me she was in protectoress mode.

Who was I kidding? Four months in she moved back full time and her new, happy self disappeared in favor of the old. The only times she laughed or smiled was when she didn't see me looking. While staring at my growing belly.

Charlotte continued to guide me down the stairs while I tucked one hand under my ginormous protuberance and begged the nugget to just freaking hurry up already.

Gram sat, knees bouncing, at the kitchen table, faded blue eyes bright, a tight grin on her face. Shenka stood next to her, arms wrapped around herself, also smiling. They would have been in the room with us, if I allowed it. But after being examined countless times by the kind-hearted Lula while a gallery of anxious family tried to hover and watch, I put my foot down.

One at a time. That was it. And today had been Mom's turn.

You'd think they had never been around a pregnant woman before.

Galleytrot lifted his big head from the floor, red flames lighting his black eyes as his tongue lolled out the side of his mouth. "Is it time?" His big tail thudded on the ground twice, only falling still when Mom shook her head with a smile so tragic I felt like I'd failed.

Give the pregnant chick a break, would you?

Sassafras licked one paw with careful attention as he spoke. "The boy is too nice to make demands," he said. "Just like his father."

Everyone in the room held their breath. Like Sass bringing up (my dead husband) Liam would make the world explode. They froze, stared at me. While I smiled and, with Charlotte's silent help, bent to kiss the top of Sassafras's head.

"With you, Gram and Mom feeding him power and your influence," I said, "I'll be surprised if he's not more Hayle than O'Dane."

Exhale. How funny, my family. So protective.

I loved them for it.

And yet, the ache of Liam's loss had faded with time, mostly thanks to the little person I carried around. As Charlotte eased me into a chair, I began to worry maybe once the peanut was born my pain would return.

"The baby is perfectly fine," Lula said. "And although you're now two weeks overdue, I have to assure you such timing is completely normal for a first pregnancy."

I nodded, silent now myself. Maybe he'd just stay in there forever. And keep me from my grief.

But no. I had to have him, let him out. If only so I could finally be free to go after Ameline Benoit.

And pay her back for making me a widow. Just before I went after Max, my supposed drach friend and gave him a piece of my mind—and magic. Then, Iepa. Light Fate.

So many people to thank for their participation in the loss of the man I loved.

I sank into my fury, feeling it tighten my body, my tension rising so swiftly I choked on a breath.

Nugget chose that exact moment to wake up and begin babbling.

Nonsense stuff. An endless stream of chatter. Muttering, giggling, cooing. Which drew Mom, Gram, Galleytrot, everyone, like a herd of nosy cats, all their power reaching for him at once.

And instantly dissolved the hate growing in my heart.

Every time this happened, I almost protested my family's eagerness to embrace the baby. My son needed his space, didn't he? And I never seemed to have him to myself. But the love that poured out of him, the welcome he always greeted everyone with, grew with each contact until I had to just sit back and allow it.

Lula's mind touched mine as my crazy family interacted with my unborn son. Like I was just some organic bassinet.

He will be remarkable, she sent, her power soft and sweet. *Already is, Syd. I think you're going to have a very powerful child on your hands. Tempered with the kindness of his father.*

I *think so, too.* Stupid tears. Beat it. *What if*—

Yeah. I was the Queen of Blurts.

You will be an excellent mother, Lula sent, firm and supported with a surge of magic. *You don't have it in you to be otherwise. And with all the support*, she grinned like it was freaking funny or something, *you have around you, I know the child will never want for anything.*

He already had a collection of baby clothes and toys so big it took up most of my bedroom.

My egos wriggled and whispered to the baby even as Mom and the others retreated. Nugget spun sideways abruptly before going back to sleep with a contented mental sigh. The girls had been amazing, thankfully, keeping watch over him as they'd done for me, allowing me to sleep, knowing he always had a guardian with access to power watching over him. Aside from the ones outside my body, that was.

"I'll be back tomorrow." Lula stepped away, heading for the door. Waved to me. "But I'm at your call if you need anything."

I waved back in thanks, wishing my fingers didn't look like sausages attached to a slab of ham, wondering at my own vanity at a time like this. Mom turned back, beaming, hands clasped under her chin.

"Let's go for a walk, shall we?" She was convinced exercise was the key to encouraging the peanut to leave my body at last. Had read it in some baby book for normals. Despite knowing the only thing we could do was wait.

Just thinking about stumping my way around the block with my over-protective werefriend and the trail of Persian, black hound, grandmother in fuzzy socks and various other assorted coven members who popped up out of the woodwork with fake surprise on their faces made me shudder.

Not to mention the fact I didn't think I'd make it without my knees giving out.

"I'm good," I said. I really didn't mean to be surly. And felt bad Mom's face fell. How they all stared at me, waiting.

Expecting me to pop. Right. Then. And. There.

Argh.

When Gram and Sassafras's magic reached out to the baby, I had enough. Shoved myself out of my chair with a groan. Shook my head when Charlotte tried to take my arm.

"I just need a few minutes alone," I said. Growled,

actually. Spun—not gracefully, but I managed—toward the basement door and waddled toward it. A heavy, furry body pressed to my side, Galleytrot glaring up at me.

Fine. Whatever. I leaned on him as we descended into the darkness, trying not to resent every step.

about the author

Everything you need to know about me is in this one statement: I've wanted to be a writer since I was a little girl, and now I'm doing it. How cool is that, being able to follow your dream and make it reality? I've tried everything from university to college, graduating the second with a journalism diploma (I sucked at telling real stories), am part of an all-girl improv troupe (if you've never tried it, I highly recommend making things up as you go along as often as possible). I've even been in a Celtic girl band (some of our stuff is on YouTube!) and was an independent film maker. My life has been one creative thing after another—all leading me here, to writing books for a living.

Now with multiple series in happy publication, I live on beautiful and magical Prince Edward Island (I know you've heard of Anne of Green Gables) with my very patient husband and multitude of pets.

I love-love-love hearing from you! You can reach me (and I promise I'll message back) at patti@pattilarsen.com. And if you're eager for your next dose of Patti Larsen books (usually about one release a month) come join my mailing list! All the best up and coming, giveaways, contests and, of course, my observations on the world (aren't you just dying to know what I think about everything?) all in one place: http://smarturl.it/PattiLarsenEmail.

Last—but not least!—I hope you enjoyed what you read! Your happiness is my happiness. And I'd love to hear just what you thought. A review where you found this book would mean the world to me—reviews feed writers more than you will ever know. So, loved it (or not so much), **your honest review would make my day**. Thank you!